– The Writing of History –

A Novel

Stephen Douglas Hayes

Order this book online at www.trafford.com/07-2802
or email orders@trafford.com

Most Trafford titles are also available at major online book retailers.

Note for Librarians: A cataloguing record for this book is available from Library and Archives Canada at www.collectionscanada.ca/amicus/index-e.html

ISBN: 978-1-4251-6156-9

www.trafford.com

North America & international
toll-free: 1 888 232 4444 (USA & Canada)
phone: 250 383 6864 • fax: 250 383 6804
email: info@trafford.com

The United Kingdom & Europe
phone: +44 (0)1865 722 113 • local rate: 0845 230 9601
facsimile: +44 (0)1865 722 868 • email: info.uk@trafford.com

10 9 8 7 6 5 4 3 2

For

Leo Braun, who lived it.

Jack Arnot, who taught it.

And what should the historical testament of Polish Jewry be? The clanking of arms, like everyone else, or the power of the spirit? The testament of the heroic warrior or of the saintly martyr?

Even more important, everything depends on who transmits our testament to future generations, on who writes the history of this period. History is usually written by the victor. What we know about murdered peoples is only what their murderers vaingloriously cared to say about them. Should our murderers be victorious, should they write the history of this war, our destruction will be presented as one of the most beautiful pages of world history and future generations will pay tribute to them as dauntless crusaders. Their every word will be taken for gospel. Or they may wipe out our memory altogether, as if we had never existed, as if there had never been a Polish Jewry, a ghetto in Warsaw, a Maidanek. Not even a dog will howl for us.

But if we write the history of this period of blood and tears—and I firmly believe we will—who will believe us? Nobody will want to believe us, because our disaster is the disaster of the entire civilized world...we'll have the thankless job of proving to a reluctant world that we are Abel, the murdered brother...."

ALEXANDER DONAT
The Holocaust Kingdom

Hear O Israel, The Lord our God is one Lord.
And thou shalt love the Lord thy God with all thy heart,
and all thy soul and all thy might. Deuteronomy 6.

Chapter 1

The old Mercedes turned off the Autobahn and struck north towards the mountains. The Bavarian countryside was every shade of green and the landscape seemed to burst with energy. Since they had left Munich the driver and the gentleman sitting bolt upright in the rear seat had chatted about the Germany of today. It was 1952, almost seven years since the defeat of Germany, and already the outward signs of that debacle were disappearing.

The car turned into a long tree-lined drive which led up to a large white house. It stopped in front of the main door and the driver stepped quickly around the car and opened the rear door for the older gentleman. The driver's heels clicked as the older gentleman stepped unassisted from the rear seat. The two of them stood for a moment admiring their surroundings. Flowers were everywhere; lining the white pebble stone walk leading up to the front door; under the trees of the drive; festooned in window boxes about the house. Another older gentleman stepped quietly out of the house and joined them. The driver's heels clicked again and he stiffened into a military attitude of attention.

"Ahh, Gunther. How good to see you again." The gentleman from the house extended his hand. The passenger from the Mercedes shook hands warmly.

"My General," he said. "You remember my old driver, Kurt Eber?"

"Of course. When you have unloaded the luggage my cook will show you the rooms."

Kurt unloaded the bags and made his way to the back of the house. He introduced himself to the cook.

Gunther and the inhabitant of the house entered the study together and sat opposite each other in two large matching chairs that were placed in front of the fireplace. They sat quietly for a few moments. Finally Gunther spoke.

"You intend to go through with this? You will allow me to write your biography for the British?"

The other man nodded.

Gunther took a small tape recorder out of his attaché case and clicked it on. His face still evinced disbelief.

A small glass showcase hung on the wall. It was the only clue in the study to the identity of the owner of the house. Lying on a velvet cushion was the Knight's Cross and next to it the Baton of a Field Marshal in the German Army.

"Shall we begin?" Gunther smiled and thought to himself that this wasn't really happening. After seven years of silence and a mystical sense of mystery, the man sitting so calmly opposite him had decided to talk about the war. This man had been the Military Commander of Berlin from1932 through 1938. He had commanded Army Group South at the invasion of Poland in 1939. He had commanded Army Group Center during the battle of France in 1940. He had commanded Army Group South at the invasion of Russia in 1941 and he was the commander of the Western defenses prior to the final defeat of Germany in 1945. His name was Karl Rudolph Gerd von Runstedt.

The man with the tape recorder was Gunther Blumentritt. For many years he had served as chief of staff for von Rundstedt and then at the end of the war he held commands of his own.

"Let me explain further." Rundstedt settled in his chair. "As you know, for many years now the press and sensationalists of every sort have been after me for my story. I don't know why but I have always enjoyed an immense popularity both in Europe and abroad. I was the subject of an American magazine cover story in late 1944, and the British papers have always treated me with great respect. I have steadfastly refused all requests and demands for my story. I have insisted on standing on my record, and on statements I made to the British in my three years of detention after the war. I have been sheltered away here with my flowers and now that I am approaching death I have this impulse to talk."

Blumentritt stirred in his chair and started to say something and Rundstedt raised his hand quickly. "No, no my friend. Hear me out. This is important. I cannot talk like this to anyone else in the world. You as much as any should know. You have understood my restraint and moderation so you will believe me all the more. It is as if God has willed me to speak now because I was the witness. I was there in Germany from the beginning. I saw it all as it happened. Do you remember Canaris and the warning he gave to Keitel in 1939? How we, the Wehrmacht would be held responsible; and how von Treckow would say that not only us, but our sons and our sons' sons, would suffer this guilt. Because it was Germany's guilt."

Blumentritt sat forward in his chair and dared to interrupt. "I will not sit here and listen to you do this to yourself. We acted with honor. We upheld our tradition. No one could have done more in our position."

Rundstedt replied calmly. "We are much too old for honor.

The only honor available to us was death. We both knew it then and we know it now. I repeat. I am nearing death and it is as if I have no control. It is as if God has directed me to speak. As if..."

Rundstedt let his last thought hang in the air, tantalizing and incomplete.

"Yes?" Gunther was forced to say.

Rundstedt smiled. "I was going to say something else, but then I stopped myself, afraid you would misunderstand. I was going to say that I feel as if at last I have found the death I should have accepted during the war. Then I remembered the old Christian saying, 'You shall know the truth and the truth will set you free.'"

Blumentritt clicked off his tape recorder and slowly rubbed his forehead with his fingertips. "Oh, my General." He repeated softly to himself several times.

In the kitchen, Kurt the driver, and Anna the cook and housekeeper, were enjoying a second cup of coffee.

"Have you been with the Field Marshal long?" Kurt inquired.

"Only two years now. But I have been with the family all my life." She was a woman in her early forties. She was not fat, but large and strong. She had a rosy complexion and an infectious smile that threatened to break into a laugh at the slightest invitation.

"We shall be here a week or more." Kurt yawned and surveyed the kitchen.

"What are they visiting about?" Anna wanted to know. "For the past month Herr Rundstedt has been nervous and irritable. The other day he had me get out his old uniform for him. He never put it on. He just sat and stared at it." She shook her head as she pushed her hair behind her ears.

Kurt gave her a knowing look. "You will learn. These generals." He nodded wisely. "Like children. Come, show me the rooms and I will unpack our bags." And then as if he had just remembered her question. "It's the war. They are going to talk about the war. My old commandant General Blumentritt is going to write a book about the Field Marshal. They are always playing soldiers, these generals. You will learn."

"Where shall we begin?" Gunther Blumentritt switched his tape recorder on. "As you know I will include a short history of the Rundstedt family. Perhaps in your own words you would tell me something of your family."

Rundstedt smiled and relaxed, his voice dry and efficient. "We have traced our family back to 1109 here in Germany. In the Harz Mountains. My ancestors were soldiers and administrators from the early part of the 14th century until today. Rundstedts have served both Saxon and Prussian Kings with honor. I knew the late Kaiser in my youth. My father served Bismarck under the elder Moltke. I served in the war in 1914 in both the West and the East. I spent some time in Hungary and I had a chance to see the old Austrian army first hand. I was sympathetic to the officer corps. Their uniforms and their use of pomp and display were magnificent. It was obvious that they were hopelessly out of touch with hard military truth. But it was in Russia that I learned my real lessons. I acquired the most profound respect for the Russian soldier. Tactically the Russians have never been our match. But as I grew older I became more and more convinced that Russia could never be conquered. The geography and the space will defeat the most massive armies."

Rundstedt arose and paced in front of his chair. "Before the war I had often thought that when the young Kaiser threw Bismarck out of office in 1890, it was his greatest mistake. Bismarck was more than Germany. He was Europe itself."

As Rundstedt talked, Gunther had the feeling that not only was his old commander unburdening himself, but he was searching for meaning, not only in his own life, but in the German nation as a whole. Rundstedt was seeing the world and the vast sweeping changes of history as a series of strategic moves, and if he could lay it all out on a map in front of him he could understand it. Gunther smiled to himself and switched off the tape recorder. The clock in the hall tolled the hour.

Anna opened the door to the study and stood quietly, listening to the last of Rundstedt's talk without hearing it. When Rundstedt stopped and acknowledged her presence she curtsied automatically.

"And what time would you like to dine?" She asked.

"At nine as usual." Rundstedt replied. She nodded and went back through the door as quietly as she had entered.

"But we did not understand that then." Rundstedt continued. "All through the decades on either side of the turn of the century, we younger officers helped to create the environment whereby Wilhelm the Second could engage in the rash of activity that led to the events of 1914. We felt the world was ours. That the twentieth century belonged to the German people and we were to lead them to glory, by the grace of God. We always felt that God was with us. We were the inheritors of the Holy Roman Empire, and the days of the second Reich were the days of our youth."

For the first time that afternoon Rundstedt's eyes glowed from within. He smiled from his heart and his voice rose out of the flat unemotional pitch he managed to register when describing even the most heartbreaking experiences.

"Gunther, you remember! To be a member of the German officer corps. In 1905, I think it was 1905, when I was a young regimental adjutant. I qualified for admission to the military academy at Berlin and I was posted there for three years and as you know my position in the army was assured. This afternoon that I remember I had taken a first in tactics and my son was just two years old. Louise and I were out for a stroll on the Unterderlinden. Von Moltke and the small entourage that was with him happened to be out walking on this same afternoon. But he was on the opposite side of the street. My wife noticed him when he was still some distance away and she whispered to me that the senior general in the army was approaching. She indicated to me that we should cross over to his side and my first impulse was to do so. But something came over me then. It wasn't pride or stubbornness. It was something finer and deeper. It was a sense of God. Bear with me, Gunther. I may repeat myself. I thought at first that I would cross the street. There was no harm in this. The young Lieutenant and his wife out for a stroll on a balmy Sunday and he should happen to meet his Commander-in-Chief; perhaps their eyes would meet, a quick nod and a short word or two. Careers have been made on less. But God touched me then. I would not cross the street. Louise was taken aback. She thought I was being pig-headed and arrogant. " No.!" I said to her. "We will walk on our side and von Moltke will walk on his." God had blessed me with His presence. I said this to myself. I am Gerd von Rundstedt, Lieutenant, 83rd regiment. I believe in God and the virtues of perseverance and hard work. If the course of my career can be influenced because of a chance encounter with von Moltke, then everything in which I believe is subject to this same whim. Then my God would only be a prestidigitator who can fool anyone, including himself. I was doing my duty. In my mind the harvest had to be good because the tilling and the sowing were being done as well as humanly possible, and I resolved then to live my life on principle , and to keep myself out of the hands of the laws of accident. We walked on past on our side of the street. One of the officers who was in the Field Marshal's party called my name just then. 'Rundstedt, please.' I turned and I was looking directly into the sun and I had to shade my eyes to see. There stood the Field Marshal himself. He had crossed the street to speak to me.

"Our congratulations, Lieutenant. We just saw the result of the tactics examination. We feel justified in having selected you for the academy."

"I could say nothing. I was so overcome. All I did was nod and there was an embarrassed silence.

"You are the heart of the army." Von Moltke continued with a few platitudes. Finally he smiled at me and left, continuing his walk.

"That evening I wandered down to the officers club after dinner and the talk was all about Moltke stopping to congratulate me on the street. I stood a round of drinks and I thought of my wife and son and serving on the general staff of the German army when my schooling was over and how God had a hand in my affairs because I had believed in Him. That was the happiest night of my life because I knew then that as long as I conducted myself as a German officer and as long as I stayed in the tradition and did my duty, I would be in His hands. "Do you understand me? I had found my haven and my rock."

Blumentritt nodded. "I know what you are saying. Always in Germany we have understood this connection between God and each individual life. We have known God as the God of history."

"Exactly. Since the days of Martin Luther, Germany has been the vanguard of religious thought. My thoughts tend to a mystical sense of mission for Germany. I cannot help myself. I aligned myself, my very being with the German army whose fate was inextricably aligned with the German people and when I knew that God was directing my affairs it became simple to then have Him direct the affairs of the German nation and thus, all of history."

Rundstedt paused and stared into space somewhere outside of Blumentritt's scope, thinking out the rationale that had motivated and protected him for three quarters of a century. Blumentritt switched the tape recorder off.

"Of course none of this will go into the book. And now commandant, I would like to change for supper."

Rundstedt nodded at him. "Yes, the book." As if he just remembered why they were talking of these things.

Anna appeared at the door and led Herr Blumentritt to his room. Rundstedt sat by himself for a few minutes. Kurt Eber then entered the study and seeing Rundstedt sitting there he stepped back quickly and tried to excuse himself.

"Please Kurt. One moment. You were with us since the beginning."

Kurt nodded. "Yes, Field Marshal. I served in the Berlin regiment under your command from 1936 to 1938. Then I was transferred to the 77th and in 1939 I was selected as driver for General Blumentritt. I have been with him since."

Rundstedt nodded and smiled. "And you are well now?"

Kurt continued. "My wife was killed in1938. My sister and her husband survived the war and I live with them in Berlin. I am comfortable and I have no complaints." Kurt folded his arms across his chest and stared blankly at Rundstedt.

"Tell me please," Rundstedt leaned forward in his chair and tried to draw Kurt into an intimate conversation. "You think of all the mistakes, all the things we did that we might have done differently. You can talk to me freely. We are no longer soldiers here."

Kurt answered directly. "No, I have no regrets."

"Perhaps you misunderstand me. I want to know what you think of us. We were in charge and we led you into disaster."

"As I said. I have no regrets. We lost the war because we bit off more than we could chew." Kurt smiled. "And then there was Herr Hitler."

Rundstedt settled back in his chair and dismissed Kurt with a nod. "Thank you, Kurt." He smiled at the driver. "Bit off more than we could chew." He repeated.

Downstairs in the kitchen Anna was curious. "What did you say to Herr Rundstedt?"

Kurt shrugged. "Nothing. What should I say to him?"

"Don't be so taciturn." She poked him good-naturedly and smiled broadly. "Tell me what he asked you?"

"He wanted to know what I thought about the war."

"And did you tell him?"

" I told him that we had bit off more than we could chew and that the real problem was Herr Hitler." Kurt lifted the cover of a great steaming pot of lamb and vegetables that sat on the top of the stove. The rich aroma filled the room and Kurt sat down and propped his feet onto the chair opposite. "While those two are talking and explaining and justifying the war, if you should want to know what really happened, you ask me."

Anna opened a bottle of beer and poured a glass for herself and Kurt. "It will be so nice to have some company for a time."

The next morning Rundstedt continued with his narrative. "When I think of those early years, from 1919 on, I see Germany stretched on an immense rack. Communism on the one side and Fascism on the other. The extreme left and the extreme right. There was no middle ground. There was a middle class but it had no voice. No political party could survive between those two rival factions. Germany was polarized after 1918 and no other voices could be heard. We in the Reichswehr were always on the political right. We never wanted an informed mass of people which would serve as the basis for a great people's army. We could never have wanted that. We were the elite. We felt, even after the defeat in November of 1918 that the officer corps of the Reichswehr was the finest in the world. How could we come to any sort of terms with Communism? It was all so alien to our nature. So we supported the political right by standing by and giving our tacit approval to the Free Corps. They ran riot throughout Germany with our approval. That was our first great error. We always thought we could control them eventually. After all, what were they but a large group of ex-soldiers? We had commanded them once and we could do it again. I remember a night in Poland in 1939. We had rolled up the southern flank and I stayed at my command post late, admiring the series of engagements that had just taken place; and feeling immensely satisfied with the total operation that was drawing to its successful conclusion. My adjutant, my driver and myself left headquarters when we passed a detachment of Himmler's Einsatzgruppe. The temperature was almost freezing. This SS platoon was marching in front of us. They wore their summer uniforms and they all had their sleeves rolled up. As if to say, so much to you, to the cold. I was thinking what fine troops they would be. After they passed, my driver made a short, derogatory remark and he spit out the window in a gesture of contempt. Then it dawned on me that these troops were defying not only the weather, but the world also. Then a second disquieting thought entered my mind. No one in the Wehrmacht had control of these troops and my mind flashed back to 1919 when we allowed the Free Corps to run wild through Germany for political reasons."

"What are they doing here?" I asked my adjutant, and he looked at me as if I had been living in a shell and he didn't answer right away. Finally he said, 'Himmler's men. They are for political and counterespionage purposes.'

"I put them out of my mind then as I had put the Free Corps out of my mind twenty years earlier but what had happened was obvious. The Free Corps had become the Storm Troops and then the SS and the Totenkampf Units and when we wanted to stop them we couldn't because they could always say; 'but it was we who have always done what you wanted us to do and without us there is no Wehrmacht'. And we who choose to remember have to shake our heads and agree with them. We endured them and used them, right from the beginning. We thought they are not beating up respectable people. They are not harming good respectable middle class Germans. When your country is threatened by anarchists and Bolsheviks you must employ all means possible for your own protection.

"The other important thing about the early twenties was the total unpreparedness, the bankruptcy of the German nation to produce political leaders who were neither charlatans, madmen nor clowns. Bavaria had a Chancellor who declared war on Switzerland. Then there was an Economics Minister who proposed a system based on vanishing currency. His name was Gesell and his theory was called Schwundgeld. All paper money would automatically lose a percentage of its face value every week. This would stimulate spending and strengthen the economy. The same government had a Foreign Minister who had recently been released from an insane asylum. This happened in Bavaria where since the days of the two Ludwigs, politics were a little crazy. In Berlin it was as just as bad. For a time all of Berlin was under the influence of Joseph Weissenberg. He thought he could communicate with the dead and he claimed to be holding séances with Bismarck. Then there was Ludendorff with his miraculous Tausend who were going to save Germany by turning baser metals into gold. And all the while the Weimar government held on. We in the army were convinced we were still in control. We had no politics. We would stay on the sidelines and then just support the winners, no matter who they turned out to be. That way we could never lose. In 1925 when Ebert, the first President, died, we thought we had the nation in our grasp. Hindenburg was elected President and we were back in power. That's how much the army understood politics in Germany between the wars. We sat and watched and did not believe. The Free Corps and the extreme right produced only one sort of man capable of leading them and he, naturally enough, was more crazed, more insane than they. All of the illustrious strategists in the army, myself included, were outflanked by a handful of street fighters. This all happened in the twenties and we thought we had won something. We were happy to have saved Germany from Communism when actually we had lost. We should have been trying to prevent a strong and unified Russia from coming into existence. Considering all the paths that Russia could have taken between the 1920's and today, the only event that would guarantee a strong and united Russia was our madness when we attacked them in June of 1941. You see it has all run together in my mind. I can see it as a whole now. From 1919 to 1945. It all seems so logical and preordained, as if we were really in God's hands."

Blumentritt moved uneasily in his chair. "I am sorry. This talk of God makes me uneasy. I am a devout Catholic and I do not take God lightly. I do not think he moves in and out of the affairs of men as easily as you say he does."

"You know I mean no offense. Did you know that it was regular army and naval officers who killed the two communist leaders, Rosa Luxembourg and Karl Liebknecht. Liebknecht was murdered by the navy, and Luxembourg by the army. Noske gave the orders. He was a politician who tended to function like a paid assassin. Waldemar Pabst was the officer in charge. Pabst is still alive, you know. He's a greatly respected citizen. But I don't intend to impugn his integrity. The total Wehrmacht acquiesced in much worse. Pabst went on from there and made himself the indispensable man, if you had a right wing coup in mind, anywhere in central Europe.

"After the leftists had been crushed militarily it only remained for the courts to then crush them judicially. I doubt if there were five cases from 1920 to 1932 which were tried in German courts, and wherein a Free Corps member, or a Nationalist was convicted. Justice ceased to exist in Germany in 1920, not in 1933, as so many believed. When we, the German officer corps, decided that the Free Corps were to be allowed carte blanche to deal with the left, we took with us the total German establishment. The doctors, lawyers, judges, magistrates, and the bulk of the middle class. Gunther, I tell you, we may not have liked it, but we created National Socialism. And we must accept all the consequences."

Anna poured Kurt another glass of thick black lager. Kurt nodded his approval.

"Tomorrow morning I'll drive into town and purchase

some strudel for you. That bakery there is one of the best in Germany." Kurt said.

"Herr Eber. I make the best strudel in Bavaria." She laughed aloud.

The little bell which was used to summon her to the dining room rang then, and she pushed through the swinging door. Kurt finished his lager and was drawing himself another when she returned.

"The Field Marshal asked me to tell you to go into town in the morning for some apples and flour." She laughed. "He wants me to make some strudel for the guests."

"Are they through for the night?"

"They are finished. Herr Blumentritt has packed his tape recorder. They were talking about Berlin in the twenties. After the great war. Were you there? I've never been to Berlin. I've been to Munich a few times. I've been out of Bavaria only once in my life."

"Oh, I was in Berlin, all right. In 1922 on my twentieth birthday. I had joined the army in the spring of 1918 when I was only sixteen. I always looked older than my age and I was very handy. I could fix anything. I was in the motor brigade of the general staff when the war ended, so I was allowed to stay in the army."

"Did you like the army?" Anna asked with a certain amount of naiveté in her voice.

Kurt laughed. "Like it? I loved it. In 1922 when I was posted to Berlin it was the grandest time of my life. Berlin was the happiest city in the world in the late twenties. The best part of being a soldier was the total sense of irresponsibility one had. You see my little strudel, our responsibilities in the army were so clearly defined that when our duty was done we were free. That is what soldiering is all about. Freedom. What civilians and most officers, especially general staff officers, never learn is what all born soldiers know. A soldier is not a man who likes to fight. He is a man who has made peace with the world. He never troubles himself about ambition or success. Life for us in the ranks was much simpler than that. We had certain prescribed duties to perform and once we put in our time and did these tasks, nothing else was asked of us. I had my days, Anna, and Berlin in the twenties, those were the days. And nights." Kurt laughed aloud.

"Let's not forget the nights." Anna blushed and laughed with him.

Kurt inclined his head toward the study. "They never understood another simple fact. Even when someone is in charge, there are certain areas, always, where no one is in charge. So to think you can control and direct events is stupidity."

Kurt propped his feet up, leaned back and lit up a cigar. "Do your duty, love your fellow man, and let the world go hang."

The tiny bell rang and Anna started for the door. Kurt winked at her. "Perhaps later I will help you with the cleaning up and then we will take a little drive. After they have gone to bed."

Anna smiled at him. "So now I am your little strudel."

The dinner table was cleared and the two generals retired to the salon where they had their brandy and a cigarette. "I tell you Gunther, I cannot get the past out of my mind. But I feel better now, having you here to help me talk about it. I hope you can stay the full week."

"And longer if necessary. Now the children are grown and gone there is nothing to prevent my staying until you are satisfied that we have enough material for the book."

"Ahh yes, the book. I had forgotten about the book."

Blumentritt continued. "The book shall concern itself only with the military aspect of the war. There will be no mention of your political or social views. The book will only repeat what you have already told the British."

Rundstedt nodded in agreement. "You know, when my son

died in1948 and I was still in that British jail, Field Marshal Montgomery was kind enough to have me flown back to Germany so I could be with my family. He asked me that day about Auschwitz. I tried to tell him how the full horror of Hitler's solution to the problems in the East was as much a shock to us as it was to him. He could not understand how the German general staff could be so misinformed about such matters. But then how could we expect him to understand the Germany of 1919 through 1945 when we who lived through it hardly understood it ourselves?"

They finished their drinks in silence and as they started upstairs Blumentritt said, "Old leader, I can see what a courageous thing you are doing. Still today I cannot entertain certain thoughts when I realize my own culpability..." Gunther let the thought trail off and the two of them retired for the evening.

Chapter 2

"The Spartacist revolution was defeated by the Free Corps in 1919 and then the Kapp putsch was put down by the workers the same year. Hitler came to Berlin to join forces with the Kapp group and he arrived at the Chancellery at the crucial moment. All the leaders from the far right had already fled or been arrested. Hitler was saved from arrest by a warning from a Jew, of all people, by the name of Trebitsch-Lincoln. Hitler had taken part in a successful putsch in Bavaria the prior day. So Hitler returned to Munich and all the extreme right groups made Munich their stronghold. The Free Corps slowly transformed themselves into the Storm Troopers and the Stahlhelm. The soldiers returning from the front formed themselves into the Free Corps. They knew Germany had lost the war, but they never felt as if they had been defeated. They bought into Hitler's theory of being stabbed in the back by the politicians.

"As for myself, I felt the war in 1914 was lost in the opening months when von Kluck made his turn inside of Paris and that not enough force was applied to the right wing of the army. The entire general staff in 1940 was composed of generals who had been junior officers in 1914. We had all experienced the stalemate that occurred after the failure of the first battle. Most of us felt the war had ended then but the troops never felt this defeat. It was all logistics. The German soldier was victorious in Russia and Italy. In France he felt that he had at least a draw. The returning soldiers then broke into two groups, the far left and the far right. The American General Pershing commented after the war that he should have marched his army right into Berlin because the Hun does not know he is beaten. Incidentally, the use of the word Hun to describe the Germans was supplied to the West by the Kaiser."

Rundstedt paused and pointed out the window at the blooming flowers. "Gunther, can you take that thing with you?" He pointed at the tape recorder.

"Of course."

"Then come. Today we will walk in the hills with the wild flowers. Anna will pack a lunch for us and she and the driver will meet us on the other side of town. We will picnic in the field there and they can meet us and then drive us back. It is too beautiful to be inside today."

Instructions were given and the two generals started off through the woods with their walking sticks in hand.

"From 1923 to the depression in the early thirties we put ourselves to sleep. We tranquilized ourselves into thinking that the problems that had created the Free Corps would go away if we refused to look at them. So we had the Republic. The glorious Weimar Republic. Weimar was chosen as the seat of government, not because it was the home of Goethe, but because militarily it was easy to defend. This Republic was declared on an afternoon in 1919 by Philip Scheidmann. He was a Social Democrat. He was having lunch in the Reichstag when he heard the German Soviets were about to start a revolt. He quickly ran to the window as a crowd gathered outside.

" 'Workers and soldiers', he shouted to them. 'Miracles have happened. Everything for the people. Everything by the people. The old and the rotten, the Monarchy has broken down. Long live the new. Long live the German Republic.'

"You see how fast things were happening with no planning or forethought. The Republic was born because a politician shouted out of a window at a mob in the streets.

The Kaiser had abdicated, terrified that what had happened to his cousin Nicholas would happen to him. He handed the government to Prince Max of Baden, and Max immediately handed it to Ebert, another Social Democrat. Poor man, all he wanted to do was talk. I know it happened. I was there. But I still have to shake my head every time I think about it. No vote. No coup d'etat. No plebiscite. Nothing but a man shouting out a window to a mob. It was incredible.

"So we had peace in Germany for a time. But we were still angry at the West. The British blockade was not lifted from the German ports until the end of June. Almost seven months after the signing of the armistice. People were starving to death. The infant mortality rate in Germany that year was one in three. Of course we signed at Versailles. We never had a choice or a say in the treaty. Only after we signed did the British lift the blockade. And they called us beasts and barbarians. If we were Huns, what were the British and the French?"

Gunther agreed with him and they walked in silence for another hundred yards.

"But we slowly put ourselves back together. Von Seekt was the head of the truncated Wehrmacht. It was limited to only 100,000 men. Naturally we wanted to expand but we had to work in secret because of the provisions of Versailles. The man who made our expansion possible was a Jew by the name of Walter Rathenau. He represented Germany at all those conferences to make sure that Germany complied with the Versailles treaty. He also negotiated the Rapallo pact which was only a Russian-German friendship pact. But it enabled von Seekt to expand the army in secret and it led to the creation of the Luftwaffe. Von Seekt had a policy of no politics for the army. We should have given Rathenau a medal. Instead we allowed the Free Corps to shoot him. We knew about his murder in advance but we did nothing. The army would stay out of politics. He was murdered because he was a Jew and he was one of the stab-in-the-back politicians who endorsed the treaty of Versailles. This was not true in the least. We were all such good Lutherans. We should do our duty and obey the law. Luther himself had preached it. The state could do no wrong. And we should hate the Jew because the Jew was God's curse. Luther's anti-Semitism was virulent. He advocated burning the synagogues and expropriating their property and expelling them from Germany. I could very easily resolve the murder of Rathenau because it fit in with Luther's preaching and von Seekt's policy. It never bothered my conscience even though there was no justice or sense in his death. We should have given him a medal. Instead we stood by and acquiesced in his murder. But in 1939 all of my defenses left me and I..."

Rundstedt let it trail off as a cloud covered the sun briefly and they walked through a small glade of birch trees. The sun was shining brightly when they emerged into the field again. "Then von Seekt made a small mistake in 1926 and it proved to be his undoing. The Crown Prince appeared at a parade with a regiment of the Prussian Guard and the Defense Minister of the Weimar Republic used it as an excuse to get rid of von Seekt. Everyone in Germany was still nervous about the provisions of the treaty. It was a small enough incident that von Seekt could have survived if he had any sort of rapport with the politicians who were running Germany. But he had so effectively cut all his communications with all politicians that when the Defense Minister called for his resignation he left quietly. He had so effectively isolated himself and the army that when he was in need of a friend in the right place, to say a word on his behalf, there was no one to ask."

At the Field Marshal's house Anna was putting the last of the lunch into a large basket. Kurt had tied a folding table and some chairs onto the top of the Mercedes. They put the utensils, napkins and tablecloth into the car with them and they stopped in town and purchased two bottles of wine. When they arrived the two generals were not yet in sight. They set up the table and chairs and they sat under an old oak and waited.

"And where were you in the twenties?" Kurt asked. "If I had met you then, who knows? Perhaps our lives would have been different."

"Please Kurt. I was only ten in 1920."

"And eighteen in 1928." Kurt laughed with sparkling eyes.

Anna blushed. "As I said, I was here in Bavaria. Once in 1926 I went to Munich. But tell me Kurt. Were you a Nazi?"

Kurt shook his head. "No. I joined the army in 1918, before there were any Nazis. After the war soldiers were not allowed to be members of any political party. In 1933 when the Nazis came to power, I was an old veteran."

"I was a Nazi," Anna said quite simply. "In 1934 I was still an upstairs maid, lonely and unhappy. I was the lowest sort of servant. I was unmarried and unwanted. My mother died when I was born and my father was killed at Verdun. I lived with my aunt and uncle, and I had to give them whatever I earned for my keep. In the twenties the party organizers and political leaders would come here from Munich and talk to us here, and at Pemberg. Pemberg was where I was born. In fact this field here, this one we are sitting in, right here by the road crossing was where the Nazi's would hold their rallies. I joined the party right here in this field. I loved the meetings and the Strength-Through-Joy organization best.

Every weekend we had hikes and outings and rides in the country and joyous dinners.

"Aah, Kurt." She leaned against his shoulder for emphasis. "I had no social position and I was poor. There was no life for me. The Nazis were great Democrats. In the party there were no social divisions. Everyone was equal. We could get out of our petty little lives for a while and live for something grand. A new life and a greater Germany."

Kurt laughed and shook his head. "And you believed that?" His voice contained a note of mocking derision.

"Yes, I believed it. Because it worked. Life was better for us here after the rise of National Socialism. We had self-respect. That is more than I could say about life under the Republic."

Kurt sighed with regret. "I am sorry. I did not mean anything. It was so easy for us in the army to see through them. We only saw the worst of National Socialism. I never thought there was anything else except their senseless killing and their endless stupidity."

Now Anna laughed. "We were so isolated here. It was not like Berlin. Even the great depression was nothing here. We always had food and we always had the beauty of Bavaria. My poverty was not of the body but of the spirit. There were few Jews here and for me, being a Nazi was quite natural."

Kurt kissed her on the cheek and got to his feet as they spied the generals coming over a rise. "I salute you, Anna. Here in Bavaria in 1952, you are the only Nazi that ever existed."

Rundstedt and Blumentritt sat at their table and ate. Then they lingered over a glass of wine and Rundstedt took up his narrative. "It was funny the way I could make a philosophy suit the reality. I accepted the position of the army. No political actions or commitments. When the dirty work had to be done we would stand by and let the Free Corps do the job. Except when it suited us to intervene. I was a colonel in charge of a guards regiment and von Seekt called me on the phone and ordered me to Thuringia to stop a workers revolt. I remember it so clearly now. We had this same wine for lunch. And I never noted the contradiction in von Seekt, Why were we standing by in Berlin and suddenly taking a political stance in Thuringia? But I was a good soldier and things were better for the army and I did my duty without question. We machine gunned some rabble in the street and it was all over.

"Then in 1929 when the American stock exchange crashed, the bubble burst for us here also. Hjalmar Horace Greeley Schacht, the great finance minister who had restabilized the Mark in 1923, came to the fore. Our government in Weimar would pay France and Britain our war reparations with money borrowed from America. The French and British would then take this money and repay the Americans what they owed them and so the Americans by lending money to Germany were repaying themselves. Then when German loans were no longer popular in America our prosperity and the worlds, collapsed. No, I never did find out how Schacht got the names of Horace Greeley. I imagine he was an American robber baron whom his parents admired. He was a wily survivor and he was only one of three high-ranking Germans acquitted at the Nuremberg trials. One of the others was von Papen. Von Papen and Schacht were the two men most responsible for bringing Hitler to power in 1933. In 1928 the Nazis only received 3 percent of the vote and then by 1932 they were up to almost 40 per cent. Now that was one of the facts that would bring comfort to so many Germans. The Nazis never received a majority of votes in any election. Schacht controlled about ten percent of the votes in the Reichstag through a political party known as the Harzburg front. He swung these votes to Hitler and so Hindenburg had no choice but to name Hitler as Chancellor. After the failure of Hitler's aborted putsch in 1923, Hitler remained committed to gaining power by legitimate means.

And in 1933 he accomplished this, thanks to Hjalmar Horace Greeley Schacht. The question remains, if Hitler had gotten a majority of the votes in Germany, would it have mitigated his crimes? Now tell me, Gunther, was there ever a time we could have stopped him? Was there ever a time when we could have told the Austrian corporal the game was up?"

Blumentritt turned off the tape recorder and rubbed his eyes. "Yes, Herr Field Marshal. In 1938, when Fritzsch and Blomberg were deposed. In fact that very evening when Fritzsch was acquitted. We should have shot Heydrich and Himmler and then started for Hitler. It would have been easy that night."

Rundstedt nodded. "But Hitler knew we would do nothing. He remembered all the incidents from1920 on, when the army sat on its hands with a wait-and-see attitude. But perhaps you are right. Perhaps in 1938...But we are getting ahead of ourselves." Rundstedt arose from the table and walked back towards the car. "Come. Come. It is nap time. I must have my nap each day."

Kurt and Anna quickly loaded the table and chairs onto the car and bundled the glasses and plates into the large tablecloth and put them in the trunk. When they returned to the house Rundstedt and Blumentritt went to their chambers and Kurt and Anna unloaded the car and then they sat in the kitchen and talked.

"You see what they are doing, don't you?"

Anna shook her head and pushed her sleeves up above her elbows. "I only see what I am supposed to see. Your general is here visiting my general to gather information for a book."

"This is true. But there is more. There is always more. But this is not just a book. A book like this the Field Marshal would have Gunther write from the archives. It is all in the record. The Field Marshal will say nothing more publicly. But his conscience is not clear. He is talking all this out, reliving it really, so he will be able to sleep better."

Anna had started to bake as they talked. She rolled out a batch of blistering dough and pinched off a bit and popped it into her mouth. She smiled to herself in a gesture of self approval. "You are all skin and bones. Stay with me long enough and I will fatten you up." She gave Kurt a taste of the dough. "But why should he feel bad? He should be content here. I am the best cook in the Bavarian Alps. All of the big inns and hotels are always after me to come and work for them but I don't go." She ladled huge scoops of strawberries into the tarts she had shaped. "I don't go. I stay here. I am happy here except..." She turned and looked at Kurt. "Herr Eber. Don't you think I should be married? I am a good woman."

Kurt hurriedly finished his drink and excused himself to go to the bathroom. He returned and took up the conversation, changing the subject.

"The Field Marshal feels badly because of the Jews and all of the political killings and the destruction of his army. That is the worst thing that can happed to a Field Marshal. To have his army destroyed."

"That's nonsense. Why should he feel bad? He did what he could. He was never a Nazi. Even the American papers treated him with respect." Then without pausing Anna continued. "And isn't it true? That I should be married?"

Kurt almost choked on his drink while Anna looked at him directly.

It was late afternoon with the shadows lengthening when the generals reappeared in the study. Anna served them coffee and a tray of her freshly baked tarts.

"We should talk a little more of the events from1920 to 1933."

Gunther clicked on the tape recorder. "I do believe we have covered it quite well."

"Gunther, Gunther." Rundstedt said with a hint of exasperation. "I know you are concerned with this book. But I must get everything straight in my head." Rundstedt stiffened as he attempted to have his will embrace the events of the past. So he could find a viewpoint, a perspective that he could live with.

"Of course." Gunther acquiesced.

So they went over it all again. The events from the loss of the great war in 1918 until the crisis of 1932. The Free Corps, the murder of Liebnicht and Luxembourg, the Kapp putsch, the inflation. Hitler's abortive putsch in 1923, the street riots and the Weimar Republic. The political murders of Rathenau and how Hitler systematically killed off all of his opposition until finally winning the Chancellorship. He was still talking when Anna interrupted them to remind them of supper.

Anna and Kurt waited in the kitchen while the two generals ate. "He is just talking over the same things."

"I'm sure." Kurt said. "He's trying to understand where the strategic mistake was made. He is wondering how he could have won so many battles and still have lost with such finality. To not only have lost but to have suffered an absolute holocaust."

"Tell me Kurt." Anna looked at him sweetly with an implicit trust in her eyes. "What really happened?"

Kurt laughed. "It was really simple. The Germans have only believed in one thing in their lives. Power. Strength. The Nazis were the greatest application of this philosophy that Germany had ever seen. The German people had no experience with self rule. All the Germans have ever had was some strong man telling them what to do. The Nazis took charge of the streets and if they didn't like you they hit you on the head with a rifle butt. There was no subtlety to them. In 1944 a young captain on the general staff and I were held up by a train being loaded with Jews and political prisoners. My captain noticed some terrible acts of brutality inflicted on the prisoners by the guards. He approached the SS officer who was obviously in charge and he launched himself into a self-righteous lecture. This is the country of Goethe and Beethoven. We are strong but merciful. He went on in this vein for a few minutes. Then the SS officer looked at him with complete disdain. My captain was wearing the Iron Cross on a ribbon around his neck. The SS officer sneered. 'We can turn that ribbon around and hang you by it as easily as it hangs from your neck.'

"The captain came back and got into the car with me. He fingered his throat. His complexion changed color and his voice was scratchy. Does he know that I am a general staff officer?

'He knows and he doesn't care.' We finished the ride back to headquarters in absolute silence." Kurt laughed nervously. "That was all you needed to know about the Nazis. If they didn't like you, they punched you right in the face."

The next morning after breakfast Rundstedt was actually smiling at Blumentritt. "I feel better today than I have felt in ten years. I slept like a baby. I haven't been able to sleep well since before the war. Worse than the nights are those grey twilight moments just before waking. That is the worst time for me. I always feel so defenseless. If there is a judgment in this world I expect that it takes place then, in those few moments before waking."

Anna brought their coffee into the study. Gunther rifled through his notes to see where they had left off. "It is all right." Rundstedt said. "I know where I am. I will take up the narrative in 1932. We have talked the 1920's out of existence. That year I was given command of Military District Three, which included Berlin. At that time General Schleicher was manipulating promotions behind the scenes. He wanted to suggest my name to von Hindenburg for the job of Commander-in-Chief of the army. I quickly squashed this idea and instead I recommended General Fritsch and he was given the job. All through these years we were looking to Hindenburg. He had replaced Ebert as President of the Republic. He gave us strict orders. If a coup of any sort by any faction was attempted, the army was to put it down. We were to keep the streets safe. Prussia during these critical years was firmly under Nazi control. The president of the Berlin police was a civilized man by the name of Grzesinski. He was also a member of the Reichstag from one of the minority parties. Goring wanted this job for himself and Goring prevailed upon Hindenburg to have Grzesinski removed from office. I received the order to carry out this task. Because of the street riots that year Hindenburg had declared martial law and so I had full power to remove Grzesinski from office. He went quietly but not before telling me that National Socialism meant the complete and utter ruin of Germany. Events were moving so rapidly that year. Unemployment had reached 6 million and the streets were full of angry and desperate people. The streets belonged to the Nazis. They understood why the German worker was out of a job. They gave him some spirit. That was the real secret of the Nazis. They appealed to the pride and arrogance of the German people.

"I tell you, Gunther, there is nothing difficult about acquiescing to evil, and true evil is as commonplace and ordinary as sunshine."

Blumentritt nodded at the Field Marshal. Rundstedt continued. "The army became a tangible asset for Hitler. How much easier for him to use us to do his dirty work. His street gangs were part of the problem of lawlessness in the streets. So he would fix that. He would create the problem and then solve it. He acted the same way in his dealings with other heads of state. First he would create the problem and then he would solve it. I never connected the two. I was such a strong supporter of law and order and yet I had arrested the head of the police in Berlin. It never entered my mind to ask, whose law and order. I closed my eyes to the Nazi madness. Immediately after being named Chancellor by Hindenburg there was a series of murders in the Vice Chancellery. Some

Ministers were shot sitting at their desks. People would bring these problems to me and I would say, 'But this is a police matter.' And six months earlier I had arrested the president of the police. Now I can see it. I deluded myself. Hindenburg was our God and we had convinced ourselves that Hitler was a temporary irritation. Eventually we would get the Monarchy back. Von Hindenburg believed that until the day he died. We never thought to ask, 'Which Monarch?' The Kaiser was hiding away in Holland and Hitler had the job. There was a clause in the Weimar Constitution, Article 48, which enabled the government to suspend all liberties in the defense of the Reich. Hindenburg first invoked this clause and Hitler used it and never changed anything in the Constitution. The state was in danger and Hitler was its great defender. Then there was the matter of the oath. Every member of the officer corps was made to take an oath to defend the Reich with our lives. It was a sacred oath. Only now the Reich was Hitler. He had us in his box."

Anna appeared at the door and she nodded at the Field Marshal.

"Come, Gunther, another of Anna's extraordinary meals. You and your driver. You both look so pale, so thin. Things have been bad in Berlin? Here in Bavaria, even when things are bad they are good." Rundstedt and Anna enjoyed a laugh over this remark as they entered the dining room.

Kurt was in a talkative mood that afternoon. "In 1932, I married in Berlin. I was an old veteran by this time. I was the senior non-com in the motor brigade of Wehrkreis Three. The depression was in high gear and unemployment had reached chaotic proportions. We in the army were always paid and I was considered a man of substance in the neighborhood in Berlin in which I lived. I was generous. I was a sport. You know how a soldier can be. I managed to make a little money on the side. I was not an out-and-out thief, but I took things. Some car parts, a little petrol or some tires for your automobile. Just enough to meet my current demands. Driving the generals I had privileges and I was always onto inside information.

"There was a young girl who was the daughter of the people who owned the restaurant where I spent my Friday and Saturday nights. She was old enough to work at the cash register, though her father watched her carefully. I had been flirting with her for two years. Late in 1932 her father expressed his concern for her to me one evening. Her father and I were quite friendly. I asked him if he objected to my courting his daughter. He was delighted and we decided not to say anything to her in order to keep with the new spirit of things in Germany. He told his wife, and I set about winning my love with a sense of having done the right thing. Anna, Anna. She was such a pretty thing in those years. You remind me of her in some ways. She would have been your age if she was still with us."

Kurt paused again and rubbed his eyes before continuing. Anna handed him a tissue. "My little Lisa, her name was Elizabeth, but I called her Lisa, decided that yes, she would marry me. I was overjoyed and we planned a big wedding. It was a grand affair for our neighborhood. We set up housekeeping on the Meisterplatz. We were very happy. Our landlord was a Jew by the name of Bernstein. He had no illusions about the Nazis and all through the thirties he was constantly making plans to sell his property and go to America. In 1937 his daughter died and his granddaughter, a tiny little eight-year- old, came to live with him. Her name was Hannah and she and my wife became attached to each other. While I was gone about my duties little Hannah would come up and visit with Lisa and she would sometimes spend the night. Lisa would teach her how to cook and sew and she would let her help in her father's restaurant. Bernstein kept putting off the move to America and one thing or another prevented him from selling. Then, in 1938 with the passage of the Nuremberg Laws he lost his last chance. That same year it was necessary for me to go with Army Group A to Bavaria for a few weeks. This was the year of Austria and Czechoslovakia.

"I was in Munich on Kristallnacht, November 9th, 1938. I will never forget that night. It was horrible. The government gave the streets and the Jews to the old Storm Troopers that night. The army and the police did nothing. Every Synagogue and Jewish business in Germany was vandalized and their windows broken. That's why the name. The night of the broken glass."

Kurt paused and stared out the window. He gave an involuntary shudder and he went outside, still staring off at the horizon. He did not look at Anna. She wiped her hands on her apron and followed him outside, standing next to him.

"Ach.." He said in disgust. "I am sorry. I have never told this to anyone before." He wiped his eyes and he shrugged with a pathetic gesture. She put her hand on his shoulder. He nodded at her. "I did some terrible things afterwards. Maybe I am getting like them. All these bad memories."

He put his arm about her waist and they returned to the warm kitchen.

"When I returned to Berlin the following week I hurried to our small apartment. There was no one home. I then went downstairs to Bernstein's apartment and I knocked on the door. Then I saw the notice from the Gestapo that this property was now in the hands of a state appointed trustee. All Jews were outlaws and outlaws were not permitted to own property in the new Reich. After a few moments a fat man appeared at the door and told me he was now the caretaker of the property. He did not know where the former owner was or the whereabouts of the people who rented upstairs.

"I went immediately to my father-in-law's restaurant. No one had seen Lisa for a week. Her father and I became alarmed. We went to the local police station and we were greeted by bureaucratic indifference. I was in my uniform and I demanded to see the local inspector of police.

He was not available and I was directed instead to the local Gauleiter's office. There I encountered the same fat man who now lived in Bernstein's apartment. He was cordial. He did not know where my wife was, or Bernstein, or the little girl called Hannah. It was most unfortunate, but what was I, a sergeant in the Wehrmacht, doing living in the house of a Jew? I filed an official missing person's report and I returned home. No one knew, or would say anything. For the next week I was beside myself with rage and grief. A major on the general staff finally helped me. He knew someone who worked in Dr. Goebbel's office. At last from him I got the story. On that night a truck had stopped in front of our building. A gang of Brown Shirts piled out and they put a brick through Bernstein's window. Hannah was upstairs with my Lisa at the time. The gang dragged Bernstein out into the street and they were looting his apartment and kicking him around when Lisa came down. She tried to stop them. They grabbed Hannah and my wife lost control. She picked up a piece of wood and hit the man who was holding the crying and terrified Hannah. He collapsed on the street and the gang became more enraged. Bernstein, Hannah and my Lisa were loaded onto the truck. No one ever saw them again. No one knew who the men were. Hannah, being a Jew was an enemy of the state. So was Bernstein. It was unfortunate that my wife had taken up with them. After that I sold all of our belongings and I moved into the barracks at the brigade. I became like a stone."

Anna started to cut some vegetables to give her hands something to do. If she had looked at Kurt she would have burst into tears. They were both quiet for the longest time.

Chapter 3

Rundstedt had a small notebook he kept in the pocket of his shirt. He was in the habit of constantly referring to it for dates and names.

"1934. Hitler decided to rid himself of Ernst Rohm and the S.A. which had evolved from the Storm Troops and the old Free Corps. They made everyone nervous, especially us in the army. Hitler had a vision of the S.A. doing the bidding of the Chancellor but Rohm had other ideas. He wanted the S.A. to be the supreme power in the state and the Chancellor was to do its bidding. Besides the S.A. there were two other groups jockeying for power around Hitler and Hindenburg. The army and the SS. Hitler owed the most to Rohm and the S.A. so he decided to get rid of them. Hitler always rid himself of his old comrades and the people who helped him, or knew about him in the early days. By using the SS to get rid of Rohm and the S.A. he would ingratiate himself with Hindenburg and the Wehrmacht. We knew what was going to happen well in advance and our instructions from Hindenburg were clear. We were to do nothing unless asked by Hitler for assistance. Secret lists were circulated among the leadership. Everyone had a list and these lists were given to Himmler and if your name appeared on them you were shot. Heydrich and Himmler trumped up a plot against Rohm, accusing him of treason. We were quite happy with this turn of events. Our hated rival was gone. Hitler now had only us to rely on for his military needs. Hitler used the leadership of the S.A. to gain power and then he had them all executed. There were a few mistakes. Von Schleicher, who had been the head of the army, was murdered in this purge, also. I could easily deal with that. Von Schleicher had entered the labyrinth of politics. He had broken the code. Every high ranking German officer who stayed out of politics lived his life without interference from the Nazis. Shall we have a little brandy before lunch today?

"Himmler and Heydrich. Heydrich and Himmler. I always laughed when I heard Himmler referred to as the cold-eyed ruler of the SS. Did you know that Wittelsbach was his Godfather? And Goring, he was the Commandant of von Richtofen's flying circus in the great war and he was a holder of the 'Pour Le Merite'. One of the highest military honors. And Goebbels, his family was related to the Flemish Gobelins of tapestry fame. And when Himmler first formed the SS the best people in Germany fell over themselves to join. Dukes, Barons, highly placed businessmen and Princes of the Church included. And now it is impossible to find a Nazi in the entire country. But Himmler was so laughable, like a schoolboy playing at soldiering. Rommel told me that in 1944 Himmler needed money for an apartment for his mistress and he had to borrow money from the party to furnish her with a place to live. His salary as Reichsfuhrer was not sufficient to allow him to keep two houses. And there was enough money and gold smuggled out of his camps in a week to afford him anything. He never did steal anything and he never advocated cruelty or unauthorized killing in his camps. He wanted everything to be done dispassionately, out of some sort of historical necessity. He believed in Hitler's Mein Kampf as if it were a New Testament. His statement in 1942 must rank with one of the most perplexing statements of all time. Rundstedt searched his notebook until he found it. "And I quote. 'Most of you will know what it means to see a thousand corpses lying there. But seeing this thing through and nevertheless remaining decent. That is what has made us hard. This is a never recorded and never to be recorded page of glory in our history.' Did you hear that? Remaining decent. Glory. Here is another quote from Himmler. 'All in all we can say that we have completed this painful task, the annihilation of the Jews, out of our love for our people. In ourselves and in our character we have suffered no damage.' Did you hear that? Love. They did it all from love. Kurt Morgen, the SS judge, actually conducted a trial against some overzealous SS officer for an unauthorized killing of a Jew. The state is murdering five thousand people a day and Himmler is conducting a murder investigation in his own concentration camp system." That afternoon the generals lunched in silence. When they finished the meal they retired to their chambers for their afternoon rest without speaking.

Anna's curiosity was aroused and she asked Kurt what he thought had happened. "Why are they both so quiet? They didn't even look at each other during lunch." Kurt was helping to clear the table. "It's the horror. They can't relive the war without reliving the horror. Like my Lisa. For the longest time I did not know how to act or what to do about her. The senselessness of her death drove me mad for a while." "What did you do?" Anna's voice was full of concern. "How did you finally handle it?" Kurt shook his head. "At first I just drank, but that just magnified my memories of her and intensified my frustration. Then in 1939, in Poland, I was driving one night from a small village back to Warsaw. I gave an officer a lift. When he was in the car I discovered he was SS. While we were still ten miles from Warsaw I stopped the car by a grove of trees. It was a quiet night and it was snowing. I turned off the engine and indicated to the officer that I had to take a piss. I went into the woods and waited behind a tree. After a few minutes he came into the woods looking for me. I shot him in the leg and he fell to the ground. While he was trying to get his revolver out I shot him again in the arm. 'What is happening? Why are you doing this?' I shoved my light in his face and I told him about my Lisa and how she was murdered. This craziness that is taking place in Germany. It's your fault. And I want you to know that. He started talking to me as if I were a child or a madman. I could see he could not understand what I was trying to say. 'But what has this to do with me?' He kept repeating over and over. I could see his eyes were dead and he would never be able to make the connection. I shot him in the head and I drove back to Warsaw alone. I thought it would help, but it didn't. Then I came to realize that I didn't want to forget. I always want to have that spot inside me that aches like a toothache, so I will never forget. It was the only time I extracted vengeance for my Lisa."

Anna shook her head. "Being a Nazi, here in Bavaria, it was not like that at all." The little bell tinkled to signal that the Field Marshal and Blumentritt had returned to the study.

"Himmler was a laughable figure but with Heydrich at his side he was formidable. It was all a mistake, one of those small errors that affect history on a grand scale. Heydrich had been cashiered from the Navy in 1931 because of some sordid affair having to do with a jilted woman. For a few months Heydrich wandered the streets as one of the 6 million unemployed. He joined the Naval Storm Troops, a small attempt on his part to salvage his pride. He was completely apolitical and he remained so all his brief life. His wife wanted him to join the Nazi party but he cared nothing for the Nazis.

A friend of his sister's heard that Himmler was looking for an intelligence officer and as chance would have it this friend did not know the difference between a signal officer, which Heydrich was in the navy, and an intelligence officer, so he recommended Heydrich to Himmler. Himmler not only hired Heydrich but he also accepted a plan that Heydrich drew up to organize a state counter espionage service. So the partnership so fatal for millions was started. It was only in1939 that I realized to what extent they had managed to control the fate of Germany. And in controlling Germany they controlled us and made us a partner to their crimes."

Blumentritt moved uneasily in his chair. "But we knew about them all along. Why, in 1938 we, the old army, the opposition to National Socialism were planning the downfall of the Nazis." Rundstedt's eyes flashed. "No, I cannot accept that argument. We went along with Hitler in the days of victory and it was only when the prospect of defeat was in our laps that we thought of acting against him. We were not revolting against National Socialism. We were revolting against defeat."

Rundstedt crossed to the glass case on the wall, took his Field Marshal's baton out of the case and cast it quickly on the floor at the feet of Gunther Blumentritt. "I accepted my honor from Hitler. And I accepted it in 1940, after the battle of France, when we felt that the disgrace of 1918 had been avenged. Also Gunther, remember, this was after 1939 when we had seen in Poland exactly what the Nazis were to mean to millions of Europeans."

Gunther started to speak again and Rundstedt raised his hand in an imperious gesture.

"I know the arguments. I know the rebuttals, the evasions, the rationales, the half truths. None of them stand up to the test of the truth." Rundstedt shook his head sadly, his voice a monotone filled with an awful melancholy. "The Wehrmacht were perfectly willing to sit still through the Jewish purges in Germany, the suspension of all civil liberties and the slaughter of millions through Europe and we only decided to act in 1944 when we were faced with the prospect of total annihilation of our armies. There were millions of unarmed, defenseless, non-aggressive people murdered because of the invincibility of the Wehrmacht. There was no other reason. You must think of this as a battle. My life is being played out on an unfamiliar battlefield. I am still at war. In this war there are no tanks, no infantry. There is only truth and justice. And the price of victory or defeat is my soul."

Blumentritt sat back in his chair with a military bearing. "Let us continue. Perhaps I will come to see these events in the same light as you."

"Under Heydrich, the SS and the SD made their presence felt in every corner of Germany. In 1938 a fish monger in Berlin was denounced as a traitor and an enemy of the state for wrapping his fish in a Jewish language newspaper. He was carted away and never heard from again. Events like this were happening all over Germany. The beasts were in charge. Brutality and intolerance were rampant. But these were also the years of the Anschluss with Austria and the capitulation of Czechoslovakia. The German people were ready to accept numerous inconveniences for these victories. When the French did not attack us over Czechoslovakia it was the shock of my life. This was Hitler's great ability. He knew that the West was beaten and had no taste for war. All of Hitler's successes up to this point only helped to embolden him. But 1938, that was the year we should have acted. Fritsch was the head of the army and Blomberg was the Defense Minister. General Beck, the army Chief-of-Staff, wrote his memorandum telling Hitler we were convinced that he was leading us into disaster. Then Hitler knew he had to act. He forced Beck to resign and then fate played into his hands. Blomberg, the Defense Minister had recently married. His wife had been a typist in his office. Hitler was at the wedding. It turned out that she had a past. She had been a streetwalker. Imagine, a typist in his own office." Rundstedt said the last as if he could forgive her being a streetwalker, but not a typist. "Goring had a file on her. He got the whole story from Keitel who was Blomberg's son-in-law. Keitel owed his position in the army to Blomberg. So Hitler replaced Blomberg with himself and then the Nazis went after Fritsch." Rundstedt paused and shuddered. "We let Heydrich and Himmler destroy this man. The Commander-in-Chief of the Wehrmacht and the best officer I ever knew. Himmler found a thoroughly despicable character who would testify that Fritsch had engaged in homosexual acts with him for money in a Berlin subway station. It was all a pack of lies. The Gestapo made the whole thing up. Fritsch could not envisage Hitler, the leader of the German nation, employing such methods to rid himself of his Commander-in-Chief. Fritsch insisted on defending his honor. He even wanted to challenge Himmler to a duel. I was to be the second. I never delivered the challenge. Fritsch should have realized what sort of people he was dealing with and ordered out the Army. But Fritsch insisted on going through with the trial. Fritsch was completely exonerated and he was reinstated as commander of an Artillery Regiment. While this affair was going on Hitler had taken on the job as Commander-in-Chief of the Army. I learned later that Heydrich was expecting the army to march on Gestapo headquarters and he was prepared to commit suicide. But again we did nothing. And now Hitler was his own Defense Minister and his own Commander-in-Chief. I retired soon after this and I was made General Oberst and I was the senior general in the Army. I returned here and thought I would live out my years in peace." Rundstedt laughed and he and Blumentritt left the study to prepare for dinner.

Kurt and Anna drove to Munich for the evening. Two American musicals were playing at the cinema. "Fred Astaire is my secret idol." Anna confessed. Kurt smiled at her and she took his arm as they entered the theatre.

"I have been told that I resemble him."

"Now that must be why I have taken such a liking to you."

After the cinema they spent an enjoyable hour in a beer garden and then Anna fell asleep on the ride home. Back at the Rundstedt house she fixed them some coffee and they ate the strudel she had saved from that morning.

"I like Herr Blumentritt." Kurt said abruptly. "I hope they are not lying to each other."

"Why should they lie to each other?"

"Not exactly lying. More like accepting certain viewpoints that are not true. It is so strange, when you get older, little things become so terribly important. And the truth, the truth becomes paramount. It becomes a matter of life and death."

Anna smiled at him gently. "And do you know the truth?"

Kurt nodded. "Yes I do. I have trouble expressing myself. But I know the truth when I hear it. It was the truth that kept me alive after my wife was gone. Murdering that SS officer. That was nothing. Dull and stupid. Brutal but necessary. If our generals had acted as I did the Nazi madness could have been stopped. Afterwards I realized that my Lisa had died because she loved, and she did not want to come to terms with hatred. That was worse than death to her. She knew it all her life. I only discovered it later."

With a nod of his head Kurt indicated the generals asleep upstairs. "This is what is so hard for them. They are as guilty as the SS and the Free Corps and the Nazis and all the other mad groups that strangled Germany. They can sense it and they can feel their way around it, but I don't know if they will be able to say it."

Anna stood up, offended. "Herr Rundstedt hated Nazis all his life. He was never like them."

Kurt gave her a smile. "You see how difficult the truth is when your emotions are involved? Try to understand it. I can see that you love him very much. No one spends the time and energy that you do in this house for just the money." Anna cleaned off the table and she put the dishes in the big sink. She poured a fresh cup of coffee for Kurt and set it in front of him. "Those SS men were nothing like him. The Field Marshal is kind and cultured and you are impossible. There is no comparison."

"You must look at this from the victims' viewpoint. One group of people has decided that you, and your children and loved ones and everyone you know is to be shot; then does it matter if some people in the group doing the shooting are kind and cultured and some are not? No, Anna, the only thing that would matter is that someone should try to stop this catastrophe."

Anna sat down and Kurt took her hand. They sat quietly together before retiring for the evening.

The next morning, as Gunther was waiting in the study, the quiet of the house was shattered by the shrill, reedy sound of a Scottish bagpipe. Then the pipes and drums of a full regimental band filled the house. It took Blumentritt a few seconds before he realized what was happening. Rundstedt had installed speakers throughout the house and he was playing a recording. Rundstedt entered the study smiling broadly and marching in time to the music.

"I have been such a bad host. I have one of the world's great collections of military music. This is my favorite. The Black Watch. I saw them perform once in Berlin before the war. Magnificent spectacle. And here, look" Rundstedt opened a standing cabinet that was tucked away between two oversized ferns. "Here." Rundstedt slid out the long glass covered shelves of the cabinet. Each shelf was full of military insignia and uniform buttons. "See, this button was taken from a young Lieutenant in the Prussian Army during the Seven Years War. And this, this epaulette was taken from a coat worn by Bernardo O'Higgins during one of his campaigns of liberation in South America. And here, the pride of my collection. This button was worn by General Sherman on his march from Atlanta to the sea."

Rundstedt handled the buttons and military gimcrackery with care. He stowed the glass cases and took up his seat again. "It is the American cavalry and the American army commanders during the War Between the States that I admire the most. That was the time of the great generals on both sides. Lee and Jackson and Nathan Bedford Forest. Grant and Sherman. Jackson might have been the greatest general of all time. So typical of the Americans. They call a bald man Curly. Stonewall Jackson, the complete apostle of flexibility in defense or attack. His campaign in the Shenandoah Valley has always been my Bible. That and Sherman's march through the South. In 1939 when we overran Poland so quickly the press coined a term for our tactics. Blitzkrieg, they said. All we were doing was copying Sherman. He was the great genius of modern warfare. He destroyed defenses by the simple expedient of attacking where the defense wasn't. Everyone credited us with brilliant strategy and new tactics. We just implemented Sherman's tactics. Which he learned from Jackson. Poland and France were Atlanta and Charleston all over again. Perhaps, given a free hand in Russia, who knows?"

Blumentritt looked up from his notes, astonished. "Herr Field Marshal, you always said that Russia was unconquerable. The space would eventually defeat all attackers."

Rundstedt's eyes gleamed and he paced nervously around his chair. "I know, I know. But given a free hand and not having to cope with Hitler's imbecilic policies, his total amateurism and his pigheadedness. Who knows? Do not forget how good our army was in 1941. We attacked Russia knowing we were outnumbered at least two to one and still we felt superior. Never again shall the world see or know an army as great as ours. We all knew it was over after Stalingrad. Our army was defeated by two things. One, our leader Adolph Hitler, and two, the Red army which did not exist and could not have existed without Hitler's imbecilic policies. But my mind is racing ahead. 1939. Poland. I was called from retirement. Hitler and his Nazi gangsters; when it came time for the fighting, they had to fall back on us, the old professionals. We won his wars for him."

Rundstedt had to relax and wipe his brow as he remembered Hitler and the Nazis. "In 1939 the Wehrmacht announced to the civilian population of Poland that they had nothing to fear from us. The German army did not regard the populace as the enemy and we would respect all provisions of international law. Behind our backs Hitler had turned loose Himmler and his small army of killers to start the systematic elimination of the Polish intelligentsia and the Jews. He never even told us that he had made a deal with the Russians to divide Poland. We always felt so foolish when confronted by one of his fait accompli. Himmler and Heydrich had been sworn to secrecy by Hitler and when the killing started we did not know that Hitler had given them the order to annihilate civilians. We stopped it temporarily. We should have arrested the entire Einsatzgruppe that was in Poland. We could have done so many things. Instead I told Hitler I would resign if the killing didn't stop. Hitler ignored us and had me and my army group transferred to France. I put Poland and the atrocities out of my mind as I prepared for the French. But there was one thing I could not get out of my mind. To this day. One event and my life has been ruined forever."

Rundstedt arose from his chair and played another American Cavalry record, lowering the volume so it stayed in the background, a counterpoint to his conversation.

"I had heard the reports of these atrocities, these political shootings taking place behind the lines. One evening after the fall of Warsaw, General Blaskowitz asked me to attend a meeting at his headquarters. General von Worysch has a group here, behind our lines and they are murdering unarmed, defenseless civilians every day. He reports only to Heydrich and Himmler. At first I scoffed. You must be mistaken. I spoke with von Worysch myself. His group is concerned with counter espionage and the suppression of anti-German elements in the rear of the army."

"Herr General." Blaskowitz was pleading with me. I shall never forget the look on his face and the desperate intensity he managed to put into his voice.. "You are the occupation commander. You can stop it."

"Can you prove this to me?"

"Blaskowitz then summoned a young major into the room. They talked quietly for a few minutes. Then Blaskowitz asked me if I could spend the night and come with him in the morning. I agreed to stay.

"The next morning we awoke while it was still dark. We went without breakfast. We drove about thirty kilometers into the country. Two personnel carriers followed us. The weather was perfect and it was the start of a beautiful day. We drove through a small town. The dawn was just breaking, a thin silver line on the horizon. There was not a sound in the village. A German patrol was encamped in the middle of the street and a sergeant was issuing orders for the disbursement of goods and furniture being taken from an inn that dominated the main street. There was not another soul to be seen. Not a sound beside the German patrol. We continued to the other side of the town and drove another two kilometers to a small glade at the bottom of a ravine. We could hear the sporadic firing of a machine gun. The driver of our car stopped and got out of the car, signaling us to follow him on foot. At the first line of trees in the wood a sentry halted us.

"No one is allowed to enter," he said.

"He recognized the uniforms of the general staff and he was standing stiffly at attention. His face was white with fear but he stood squarely in front of us. "I have strict orders, sir. No one is to pass." He held his rifle at port arms, blocking our way.

"Your orders are cancelled," Blaskowitz said. "This is General Oberst von Rundstedt. He is the military commander of all of Poland."

The sentry saluted and let us pass.

"When we came out of the wood on the other side we were standing on the edge of a small clearing in the forest. A pit had been dug about 20 by 20 and ten feet deep. The machine gun was mounted about fifteen feet from the edge of the pit. Inside the pit there were perhaps 25 or 30 bodies, all naked; men , women and children. Standing to one side there were another 25 people. They were undressing and two SS officers were hitting them and yelling at them to hurry. When 4 or more people had shed their clothes they were pushed to the edge of the pit and the machine gun opened fire. The bodies would then fall into the pit.

"It was a scene from Hieronymus Bosch. No one screamed. There was no crying or yelling from the children. We stood transfixed for two or three minutes, unable to think or to move. A man with his wife and son and an infant in his wife's arms were led to the edge of the pit. The infant was gurgling and smiling. The mother was weeping but no sound came from her throat. The boy was about ten years old and the man was talking to him calmly and earnestly. The boy was biting his lip and it was obvious he was trying not to cry. The father's words had good effect on the boy. As they were led to the edge of the pit the boy put himself in front of his mother and the infant in a last futile gesture of protection. He glared at the machine gun as it opened fire and they all fell dead into the pit with the others.

"At this point Blaskowitz recovered his senses and he shouted out a command to the SS officer. The SS officer approached and stiffened when he saw us. Blaskowitz then ordered the German soldiers to cease the operation immediately and he threatened to have them put under arrest. We left and we made the drive back to headquarters in silence. I reached von Worysch on the telephone at once. I did not care what his orders were. The indiscriminate killing of civilians was to stop immediately. He stuttered and stammered and I told him to tell Himmler that the army would fire on his soldiers if they continued with these operations. I returned to my headquarters and shortly afterwards I was transferred to France. The real war was yet to come and we could still not understand why the British and French had not attacked while we were busy in the East. The murdering I had witnessed was explained to me by a phone call from Berlin. That small village was a stronghold of Polish resistance and there was no other way to deal with these saboteurs. That SS officer was guilty of overzealousness. I managed to put this entire incident out of my mind. But I could not keep the image of that family out of my thoughts. I would see them everywhere. I would see the father and mother with her infant and that little boy, choking back his tears and glaring at the machine gun with defiance. I would hear the rumors of the SS activity in the East and I would not associate it with that family. Those murders had created a trauma in my mind and I could not deal with it. Since the war's end, after being presented with the facts and realizing the hatred that existed toward all of Germany everywhere in the world, I never connected what I had seen that morning with what happened in Poland and Russia for the remainder of the rule of National Socialism."

Blumentritt turned off his tape recorder and put his pencil down. He rubbed his forehead slowly. "My Field Marshal, we have all had thoughts like this. We have all had black moments of guilt, both individually and collectively. Do not be so hard on yourself."

Rundstedt almost cried. "But that family. I can still see them. And the great question remains. What could that father have said to that little boy? What could he have possibly said?"

Chapter 4

Anna fell into the habit of kidding Kurt. Whenever they were alone together she would tease him. “Come now, Kurt.” She would say to him. “Admit it. I will make someone a fine wife.” She would throw her shoulders back and pull in her waist to accentuate her figure. “You must admit it is true.” Then she would catch him looking at her and she would adjust her stocking. “If we were married we would be there, together, all the time.” She would nod her head in the direction of her room.

Kurt would mutter to himself. “Woman or witch? I can’t tell. What are you doing to me?” She would laugh and he would chuckle to himself uneasily, as if he were in control of the situation.

“Were you in Paris?” She asked.

“Of course. The Field Marshal had his headquarters in St. Germain. General Blumentritt was his Chief-of-Staff while we were there. I was in Paris every night and almost every weekend. That was a lovely war. Not at all like the first one. Fast and less bloody. Herr Rundstedt insisted on being close to the front. We moved headquarters daily. We were moving so fast. There was resistance and hard fought engagements, but there was no front. Our motorized divisions raced to the channel ports and when they encountered resistance they just skirted it. It was a soldier's dream to be in that battle. Rundstedt and his aide Captain Salviati would ride to the front each day and the limit of the front was only determined by the amount of petrol our tanks could carry with them. That was the sort of attack you could call glorious. The French surrendered on the 21st of June in1940 and we spent the summer in France and as I said I was in Paris every night." Kurt gave Anna a funny look.

"I did a lot of women chasing that summer." Anna laughed as she thought she saw him blush.

"I don't want to hear about the chasing." Her eyes sparkled. "But you must tell me about the catching."

Now Kurt laughed. "It was a conflicting time for me. Here I was in France in the middle of a perfect summer and I almost fell in love again. It had been almost two years since my Lisa had disappeared and I could still not let her go. I could stand only the most casual relations with another woman. I met this young girl about Lisa's age. She was German, from Hamburg, and she had no friends in France. Her father had moved the family to France in 1937 to be closer to his business. He was a wine merchant. We Germans were very unpopular in France. This young girl and I spent much time together and I could see that she was attracted to me. But Lisa's memory would not allow anyone else into my life. Rather than lead her on, or hurt her, I invented a story about being wounded in Poland and not being able to perform with a woman any longer. As I said, I was conflicted. I still wanted to live and have relationships with women, but it was impossible for me. So I turned to the brothels of Paris."

Kurt and Anna sat in silence for a few minutes. Anna took

his hand. "I know. That sort of loss makes us do strange things. Now I will tell you a story."

"When the war was drawing to a close I was living here, in this very house. In April Herr Rundstedt came here from the hospital. He had problems, on and off since his heart attack in Russia. I had a young suitor and right after we met he joined the army and was sent to the East. I wanted us to get married and he said no. It would be best if we waited. We all thought the Russian invasion would end quickly, like in Poland and France. We were very close. We could be together without feeling the need to talk or anything. We were just compatible. You remind me of him in that same way. Then in the end of 1942 his unit was trapped at Stalingrad. I never saw him again. I have his last letter to me still."

She took an old tattered letter from her apron and held it up for Kurt to see. " Let me read it to you. You will see what an outstanding young man he was.

"My dearest Anna,

Please forgive me for not answering your last letter sooner but the fighting here has been intense for the last six weeks. All sorts of rumors abound and I imagine you at home have a clearer idea of what is happening than we do. We are only the troops, cannon fodder we call ourselves. Of our original unit of 120 men there are only 36 of us left. We are still called a company but a platoon would be closer to the truth. Reinforcements stopped arriving in October. We were inside of Stalingrad for two weeks. It is incredible how the Russians can hold on as long as they do. Each week passes and we are told that the city will fall in the morning but every morning the Russians are still there. Now they are getting stronger and we are getting weaker.

"But I do not want to tell you of military matters. Germany could conquer the world and it would mean nothing to me. I have missed you since I left Germany and I am sorry that we did not marry while we had the chance. What we were waiting for has escaped me. I hope this letter helps you to realize the depths of my feeling for you.

"Now I have something unpleasant to tell you. The censorship of the mail from this front is absolute, but I have a small hope that this letter will reach you intact. One of my comrades lost his leg last week and he is being flown out today. He promises me he will post this letter to you from East Prussia when he arrives there.

"Our Fatherland, our Germany that we have loved, is hopelessly corrupt. The things I have seen in the East are beyond description. Our Government is sponsoring murder and rapacity on a scale that numbs my mind. Someday the full extent of these crimes will be known, but for now I think it is important that someone at home should know that at least one of the soldiers whose presence in the army is making these crimes possible is raising his voice in objection. You must realize that I can make no other protest. We witnessed a shocking massacre of civilians on our march through Russia and we were told that our lives would be forfeit if we insisted on testifying to what we had seen. We were camped for a while with a contingent of the Waffen SS and those soldiers assured us that much worse would continue to occur. Every Jew in Europe will soon be dead, an SS sergeant told me with some pride. I honestly believe I shall not live the year out. Everyone in this once mighty 6th Army will die or wish they were dead. We are completely surrounded and our Fuhrer, of whom we were once so proud, has signed our death warrant by not allowing us one step back.

"I cannot deny my personal share in all of this even though it is in the ratio of one in 70 million. Still it is there. I was happy with the Nazis and I joined the army eagerly. I cannot think of evading my responsibility and I reason that by giving my life some of the debt is paid.

"It is important to me for you to know how much I love you. I live each day for your memory and I carry your picture in my breast pocket, close to my heart."

Anna's hands were trembling as she finished reading the letter. Kurt stood up and put his hands on her shoulders, comforting her. She turned and faced him taking both his hands in hers. "We were all wounded in the war. We all have scars. You and I, and our generals. What is important to remember is that we are not alone in our suffering."

"France 1940. There had been continual meetings with the entire general staff and Hitler through 1939 and into 1940. These meetings all dealt with the same problem. The real war which was about to begin with the French and the British in the West. Poland was ours and our rear was secure with our treaty with Russia. In my command there was a young general by the name of Manstein. It was his idea to attack France, not through Belgium as had been done in the First War, but through the Ardennes. As soon as I heard this idea I had my staff draw up the plans to carry out this plan. The other generals resisted this idea of Manstein's and they degraded it as impractical. They were convinced that the Ardennes forest was too great a natural barrier and it could be defended too easily. I was sure the French would assume the same. With the maneuverability of our armor and the speed with which our armies could move, as shown in Poland, it seemed to me to be the perfect opening for the coming battle.

"The general staff then managed to have Manstein transferred to an obscure post hoping this would be the end of this upstart. I kept pointing out that if we attacked France through Belgium again that the French and the British would be ready for us. Somehow Manstein managed to get his plan to Hitler and despite all the objections of the general staff his plan was adopted and carried to its successful conclusion. Hitler then took Manstein's plan for himself, deluding himself into thinking it had been his idea all along. It was Manstein and I who made the attack and Hitler took all the credit for it. This was how Hitler reached his final ascendancy over his generals.

"Now it was apparent to me and to any other astute observers that Hitler was a hopeless amateur in the art of war. He was incapable of employing this superb instrument, this German Army, with precision and economy. He issued orders which were absurd when the slightest difficulty presented itself. Every event became a crisis. At Dunkirk all we had to do was to advance another ten kilometers and we would have captured the entire British Army. We were ordered to halt by Hitler. Of all the excuses I heard put forth for why Hitler let the British go at Dunkirk, I have never heard one that made any sense. He didn't want to get our tanks bogged down in the mud? Nonsense, we rolled through worse in Poland. He wanted to negotiate a truce with England? How much easier if he had their Army to hold out to them as bait? The only thing that makes any sense is to realize that Hitler was mad and incapable of ruling a nation of 100 million souls. Later events have proven me correct in this. We were led by the nose by a madman and we, the general staff had lost our ability to act because of the cowardice we had shown in 1938 and 1939. I am convinced of one other thing. Hitler's great raison d'etre was destruction and he wanted to destroy, not only our enemies, but Germany itself. The invasion of Russia and declaring war on America insured this."

Rundstedt and Blumentritt decided to dine out that evening. They phoned ahead to a restaurant in Munich and the proprietor assured them of his discretion. Rundstedt was still well known throughout Germany and his appearance at a public place was sure to draw a crowd. Kurt pulled the Mercedes around to the front of the house and Anna sat in the front with him while the generals sat in the rear.

"It will be nice for you not to have to cook for one night, my dear Anna." Rundstedt said as they drove off.

They made the drive to Munich with Rundstedt obviously enjoying himself. He was talkative and jovial. "I got the reputation for being taciturn because of the reverence and awe with which German Field Marshals were treated. Someone was always there to quote us. It was a highly charged situation. We were like movie stars, as far as the Germans were concerned." Rundstedt shook his head with regret. "It was easy for me to forget Poland. It was the Western Front that tantalized me and supplied a fine edge to my life. I couldn't wait to get back at them. I knew one thing for sure. We would not have 1914 all over again. I was convinced of that.

"The French were convinced of the opposite, that it would be 1914 all over again. The Maginot line was nothing more than an updated, comfortable trench. A defensive position that was worthless. The French thought that if they were to spend another four years sitting opposite us they would at least be comfortable. The First World War was dominated by the machine gun and the Second by the tank. So France fell in 6 weeks and I remember thinking that now Hitler has what he wants and we will have peace. Versailles was overturned and our honor was redeemed. And then, almost casually, Hitler told us that we were going to attack Russia. We tried to dissuade him. Russia had twice our man power and an equal number of tanks. 'All lies', Hitler said. We would go through Russia the same way we went through Poland and France."

They arrived at the restaurant and Rundstedt and Blumentritt entered the front door by themselves. Kurt and Anna drove to the side door and Kurt parked the car. It was raining slightly, a dull, steady drizzle. They went into the kitchen. The cook had set a place for them at the large table in the center of the room. The restaurant was small and intimate but the kitchen was spacious. Kurt and Anna hung their coats on the standing rack just inside the door. The cook's name was Brandt. He and Kurt had known each other during the war.

"This is a great honor for us," Herr Brandt said. "The Field Marshal is a great man."

The two generals sat with dignity at a small table in the

rear of the dining room. A bottle of champagne was chilled and awaiting them and Rundstedt invited the owner and the Maitre d' to have a drink with them. The owner of the restaurant was obviously impressed.

"A great honor, Herr Field Marshal. A very great honor for us. And for me personally. I was a young captain in the 16th Regiment, Army Group South in 1941 when you retired at Poltava. That was a great honor for me also."

Rundstedt nodded and they all raised their glasses in a toast. The owner excused himself and the Maitre d' took up his position by the door. A few minutes later a man and his wife and their two children arrived. They were seated at a table on the other side of the room, away from the generals.

"Every time I think it is under control it starts again. See, there. It is them again. That family I saw murdered in Poland all over again. Everything comes back to me now. A flood of memories. Hard cruel edges. It is haunting me now. Eternity yawns before me and there is no rest for my troubled soul. I must express this memory to another human. I can get no rest. You must hear me out. It is not a confession but rather a statement about my life and my beliefs."

Blumentritt looked around and moved uneasily in his chair. "Yes, my General. I understand and I will hear you out."

They sat silently for a few minutes until the waiter appeared to take their order.

In the kitchen the cook and Kurt and Anna were enjoying their champagne. "Don't worry. We will put it on your boss's bill." Herr Brandt laughed. "Do you remember how we always fooled them during the war?"

The three of them laughed as Herr Brandt refilled their glasses. Anna could not stop giggling. "It's the bubbles." She said.

They had a sumptuous meal and for dessert, rich dark Austrian coffee and a bottle of American brandy along with Herr Brandt's specialty; a Bavarian chocolate cake.

Herr Brandt wanted to talk about the past. "In the last year of the war my wife and I thought it best if we left Munich for a while. We closed the restaurant and we moved in with my wife's sister for a time in a small town in Austria. She and her husband had a bakery in Perg, a small town north of the Danube, not far from Linz. They had a contract from the government to bake bread for a camp which was located at Matthausen. My sister-in-law obtained a special permit for us since we were to help her in the bakery, a vital job. We lived there from September of 1944 until the war ended in May of 1945. Then we thought we would return here and start to rebuild our lives.

"We found out that our permit did not mean anything anymore and we had to get a pass from the American officer in the Burgomeister's office in Perg. The American explained that we were not allowed to leave Perg and that we had to report to a work detail that next morning. The Americans were so shocked at the conditions at Matthausen that everyone who had anything to do with the camp had to work there and assist in the clean up and to work as nurses to attend to the survivors. We reported to the camp in the morning. At the camp we were confronted with a reality that has not left me yet and which killed my poor wife. My poor wife, bless her soul. She cried herself to sleep every night of her life since that day. It was not just the horror we saw then, but the stories we heard and had to believe. The thousands and thousands of atrocities that had been committed, all by Germans, in the name of the Third Reich."

Herr Brandt had to pause a moment and he poured them all another cup of coffee. "We lived ordinary lives here in Munich before and during the war. We both joined the party in 1935. We had heard the stories about what had happened in Poland but we discounted them. We agreed that some bad things had happened but not on the scale that we were now confronted with. Our Germany would never condone such acts. We knew there were Nazis that were capable of anything; but our government and our army would never permit such things. We were not barbarians. We were the most cultured nation in Europe. Our Rundstedts and our Rommels would never permit such behavior. We kidded ourselves with those thoughts for years and we closed our eyes and ears when confronted with evidence to the contrary. Then to be shocked into reality by having to work there at Matthausen. It was a death camp. My wife, bless her soul again; a saint. I always said she was a saint. She had to take care of the living dead. Men and women who weighed less than fifty pounds, still alive, having lived through that hell. They all had stories that would break your heart. Stories of the children, and the trains, and the towns that were totally eliminated from the face of the earth. Stories that would drive you mad."

Brandt paused for a moment. "If you don't want me to continue."

"Please finish." Anna said.

"I was assigned to the burial detail. There was an immense open pit which contained about 300 bodies. We had to first sort them out and then bury them. Some of the bodies were still fresh and some of them were decomposing. On a hot day the conditions were worse. But I was glad of the work. When we realized what had been taking place there we could not escape the guilt. We who had stood in the streets, wearing our red and black swastikas with pride. And when that pit was emptied there was another, also full of humans. The children were the worst. Whenever we dug up a small child. That was the worst for me. I still cannot think of it.

"After most of the work was done the Americans gave us a pass to return here and luckily our restaurant was still standing. I tried to throw myself back into my work but it was no good. Every night I would sit and watch my wife go mad before my eyes. I had to take in a partner and now he is the owner, but I don't care about that. My wife and I were never greedy. A nice living was all we ever needed, but that month in Matthausen killed my wife and I am sorry."

Brandt buried his face in his hands and started to sob uncontrollably. After a few minutes he regained control of himself but his eyes remained full of tears. "This happens all the time. I can't help it. I start to cry and I cannot do anything about it."

"We understand." Anna said and took his hand.

Herr Brandt nodded at them but did not agree. "You do not understand. No one will ever be able to understand."

Chapter 5

The next morning Rundstedt was already waiting for Blumentritt. He had been sitting in the study since dawn. Anna served them coffee in the study.

"Again, last night I couldn't sleep." Rundstedt sounded resigned to his fate. "I was the most vociferous of opponents to Hitler's scheme to attack Russia. When I was first apprised of his plan I had a good laugh. This madman wanted to attack Russia on a line stretching from Archangel in the north, to Astrakhan on the Black Sea. He wasn't going to do it piecemeal. He was going to go about it with a front that reached almost two thousand miles. When I saw that my objections were falling on deaf ears and that the general staff would have no say in the matter, I tried to do my job as best I could. I knew that if this mad scheme had any chance of success then the attack should have come from North to South. We should have secured Leningrad and forged a link with our allies, the Finns, and then started the drive South and East. Hitler insisted that the center of gravity should lie equally with me in the South and Army Group center. The Caucasus, he kept saying. The war cannot continue without the oil from the Caucasus. We never did get the oil from the Caucasus and the war raged on for another four years. That was the trouble with Hitler. He never did know what he was talking about.

"My primary objective in the first few months of the war was to encircle the bulk of the Russian forces west of the Dnieper. I thought if we could capture enough of the Russian army we would be able to force a decision on them and gain another quick victory. That was the trouble with attacking Russia. Between June of 1941 when we crossed the Bug River, until December when winter set in, we had captured 900,000 Russian soldiers. A haul that would destroy any other country in the world. But not Russia. It was a drop in the bucket. When the attack started we estimated 150 Russian Divisions and by November we had already identified over 230 different divisions and they were just beginning to mobilize. Then there was the Commissar order. Every Russian political prisoner was to be shot; no trial, no sentence, no reason. It was then that we should have turned our armies around and marched on Berlin. We did not know the diplomatic situation or the full military situation."

Blumentritt interrupted. "But, General. We did not know in those days what the army would do. The Luftwaffe and all the anti-aircraft batteries were under Goring's command. The SS was sure to be loyal to Hitler. If we tried to force a political change at this time we could not be sure if we would be obeyed. The army had increased 200 times since 1936."

Now Rundstedt looked at Blumentritt as if he were a child. "That is the same sort of apologist logic as trying to absolve Germany of any wrong doing because the Nazis never received a majority of votes at the polls. How insane that is. We could not be sure that the army would obey if we ordered it to march on Berlin, instead of Russia? The entire nation, especially the army has justified their actions with the cry, 'We were just obeying orders.' Now you want to employ the opposite reaction, that we were afraid that our army would not obey an order. We cannot have it both ways. We are hoist on our own petard."

"I see your point." Blumentritt replied flatly.

"To allow our armies to be misused the way we did was absolutely criminal. Orders were flying out of Berlin like so much popcorn. I had to laugh. I was ordered to take Rostov and secure the Donetz Basin and I had just entered Kiev, 500 miles from Rostov. I knew that some of the SS commanders could not read a map and I thought the same was true of Hitler. In Russia, despite all of our early successes, there was always that sense of doom that accompanied all of our activities. In tactics the German army was supreme, no doubt because Hitler did not bother himself with technique. But in strategy we were rank amateurs. I could see the end coming so clearly. The disposition of our armies, the uncoordinated way we attacked and established our front. A schoolboy could have seen it. As early as October of 1941 I started to advocate a general withdrawal towards the North and West. Back in the direction from which we had come. Already our lines were stretched too far and Hitler wanted me to dilute my strength further. I replied to Hitler in the strongest terms possible. In an unprecedented move for him, Hitler came east to see me. He wanted to know why I had left Rostov. I wanted to withdraw west, behind the Mius river.

"Hitler arrived at my headquarters in Poltava. With him were the Generals Brauschitsch and Halder. I tried to explain to him how Rostov was indefensible at this time. I showed him the position of the Red Army under Timoshenko. Hitler then went into one of his tirades. When he had finished I answered quite calmly while looking him in the eyes. I had no fear of him. I said, 'the responsibility for the success or failure of this operation must lie with those who devised it.' We all knew what that meant. If I had told him to not blame me for his mistakes I could not be any clearer. The room froze at this point and later Halder told me that he thought that Hitler was going to attack me personally. His two SS guards unshouldered their weapons. Poor Brauschitsch had a heart attack right there on the spot and it was the only thing that saved the situation. The ministering to Brauschitsch and the calling of the doctor caused the meeting to break up. Hitler then replaced me with von Reichenau and soon after Hitler was forced to allow him to withdraw to a position behind Rostov. The exact move I wanted to make from the start. I had a heart attack and I was given permission to retire by OKW.

"Heart attacks became the rule for the general staff that year. Reichenau died of one, and he was the only Nazi on the general staff. So I retired for a while and I came home to my records and my collections. I kept in touch with Generals Beck, von Bock and von Leeb. We had all been replaced by Hitler. As if we were the problem. About this time General Beck, our Chief-of-Staff tried to organize some resistance to Hitler. We were now enmeshed in a two-front war that we could not win. It took the generals another year and a half to agree and they finally launched into that insane plot of 20 July 1944. I held myself aloof from that operation. Our general staff had been trained to fight large scale military engagements, not revolutions. As Goebbels said after it was over: Amateur revolutionaries. And he was right. I stood aloof and held to my lifelong commitment of no politics for the army, even though I knew, better than anyone, how crazy and dangerous Hitler was. You see, when I had my confrontation with Hitler I established my ascendancy over him. He held no magic for me and I saw him for what he was. A frightened, inept little man. And I knew that he feared and respected me because I was what he wanted to become. I saw then that his SS and his SD and Gestapo were all nothing but an enormous bluff. They never had any real power in Germany. It was the army and only the army that was all powerful. Being secure in this knowledge I refused to exercise whatever influence I might have had over him. I felt I had to hold myself aloof so that I would not become contaminated by him."

Rundstedt laughed ironically. "Instead I have tainted myself beyond belief. My philosophy failed me." Rundstedt stared off into space and Blumentritt knew that there would be no further comments coming from him this morning.

After lunch that day Anna and Kurt took a walk in the field behind the house. They packed a bottle of wine and some cheese in a small sack and they walked over to the far side of the field where they sat on the grass under a large spreading elm. Kurt read from an American western and Anna had some sewing with her. They sat for half an hour, content to be out on such a lovely day and not feeling the need to speak to each other. Kurt set his book down. "I am becoming an expert on the American West. I knew a young sergeant in Russia. He had read all of Mein Kampf and he was familiar with the Nazi plan to replace the Poles, Slavs and Jews in the East with peasant farmers from Germany. Then it would be just like the American West. Instead of having to get rid of Indians we would have to get rid of all the inferior types in the East. Germany was just following in America's footsteps."

Anna looked at him dreamily. "Let's forget about Hitler and Germany for today. Let's just think about ourselves. There are enough problems without worrying about the past."

Kurt snapped at her. "You know this kind of talk makes me nervous."

Anna was nonplussed. "Come now, my little Strudel," she imitated him. "The other day when I told you about all of my scars and how my love had died in Stalingrad, I did not finish the story. There is much more. All through 1943 I kept hoping that he would be alive somewhere. That somehow he had survived the disaster. Then in 1944 a list was published of the known dead in Russia and his name was on it. I became a little like you when you learned of your wife's death. From 1944 until the war ended in 1945 I was in a state of shock realizing what his death meant to me. I thought that I wanted to die and then I said to myself, no, I will not die. There is still something possible for me. I will find another lover and have children. I will be useful.

"Then I panicked. I became so frightened. For a while in March of 1945 we thought it would be the Russians who captured Bavaria and we all thought we would be slaughtered. By this time we had all heard the atrocity stories from the East. When the Russians arrive, the men will be shot and the women will all be raped. That's all there would be to it. I was still a virgin at this time and I became fascinated by the idea of rape. It was like a watching a snake approach you. Fear and anxiety and a strange desire, all mixed up together. Then I thought, what man would want me after the Russian army was done with me? And then its opposite. What man would want a thirty five year old virgin? In late March of 1945 when it became clear that the Americans would liberate Bavaria, I was almost disappointed. The Americans did not rape the women and kill the men. I started to panic again. My God, I thought, this is worse. I was not going to be raped.

"I learned that the Russians were heading north to Berlin and in a week or two they would be at the gates. So you know what I did?"

Anna poured herself another glass of wine and stood up and patted Kurt on the head. "I made my way North in those last horrible days of April, 1945, when the roads were clogged with refugees and the SS were shooting people by the side of the road and nobody knew what was what anymore. I arrived in Berlin on April 30th, just in time to be raped by the Russians."

Anna paused and Kurt turned to look at her. He thought she would be distraught and instead she was smiling at him. "I got back here safely enough and I have just been waiting for the last five years"

Kurt looked at her with new curiosity. "What an incredible story. If it is true. And I don't know if I believe you or not."

She smiled at him and leaned over and kissed him lightly on the mouth. "Of course it's true. And don't you think I will make a perfect wife for someone ?"

They both laughed and made their way back across the field to the house.

Rundstedt put a waltz on his phonograph. It was an old fashioned, lush, turn of the century waltz. He waved his finger in the air for a moment and then he frowned as the memory escaped him. "Of course," he said shortly. "In Cassel, during my retirement, I danced one evening with the Baroness. It was this tune." He smiled at the remembrance. "She kept asking me about Fortress Europe and the West Wall. 'We are safe here of course, General.' She was waiting for my reassurance.

"With a beauty such as you no man is ever safe." Then she gave me a frightened look. But it did not matter. I was getting to be an old hand at diplomacy. In 1943 and 1944 up to the invasion of Normandy, I was the Reich's ambassador, without portfolio, to the rest of the world. I think Hitler was starting to realize how odious his regime had become and he thought to present a more humane, civilized face to the West. I was his showcase German. How can Germans be so bad? Have you met von Rundstedt? And I was an avid Nazi hater. But Hitler, crazy as he was, was smart enough. He knew I would do my duty for the Reich. He knew when the interests of the Nazis and the Reich coincided I would do my part. I remember my responses. Concentration Camps? Of course we have them. Every nation in the world has such places for criminals and anti-social types. Wholesale killing of Jews? Don't be silly. There were some excesses in Poland but they stopped immediately. Our quarrel with the west is nothing. The real war is in the East. Communism is the real menace. I regret my actions to this day.

"But in my entire collection of regrets and remorse do you know what I regret the most. After Stalingrad there was Kursk. Stalingrad we could all see coming. Everyone but Hitler saw it. There was no way to supply the sixth army. It was Goring's fault. We could have convinced Hitler to let Paulus withdraw but for Goring's boasting. He said he would supply the sixth army by air. That was the end for that hapless army and Paulus. Goring could not do it but Hitler let him try until it was too late.

"But we still could have salvaged something in the East if we could lure the Russians into one massive battle and defeat them. Then we could have pulled back our lines and save at least what we had gained. The Kursk salient. There was a bulge in our lines and Marshal Zhukov, the Russian Commander-in-Chief, rushed men and supplies into the bulge. This is my great regret.

"Not being present and in command at that battle. The largest battle ever fought in the world.

" Over two million men, 4,000 tanks and limitless space in which to maneuver. The front was over a thousand kilometers. And I was not there. We lost that battle and with it the war. Then and there. The cream of our armor was expended in that battle. We no longer had the ability to dictate when and where battles were to be fought. Hitler, in absolute control, declared to every soldier and unit in the army, not one step back. No general could move a battalion without his approval. His best generals were at loggerheads and could not agree among themselves on how to proceed. Kluge and Guderian hated each other so much they requested Hitler's permission to fight a duel. I should have been there at Kursk."

Rundstedt's eyes glistened. "I am sorry. I cannot help myself. If I had been there the outcome would have been different. I knew Zhukov well. I knew how his mind worked. I would not have fallen into his trap." Rundstedt exhaled an enormous sigh.

"But Hitler. Perhaps it is just as well. He would have frustrated any attempts to restore fluidity to the army. In my eyes, his greatest sin as a commander. He transformed our great army into a static block of granite that our enemies could just chip away at as if we were just so much stone."

Again Rundstedt shook his head. "It is all so shameful. The war is over and Europe is in ruins and the Field Marshal regrets he could not be at the battle of Kursk. Then one day in 1944 Blaskowitz came to see me."

"It has never stopped. Poland in 1939. The killing squads have never stopped. Murder on an unheard scale."

I shook my head in denial. "This can't be true"

"If you want to believe that then never ask any questions. Never inquire about the great camps in the East. Auschwitz, Treblinka, Sobribor. Never ask where it is that the SS transports go."

"I had some pressing business and I remember dismissing Blaskowitz and putting the incident out of my mind. It was like my Polish family. As long as I could keep from thinking of them, they did not exist. I had so many other things on my mind in 1944. Where were the Americans and British going to land? Rommel and I never did agree on this point. He wanted to keep the Panzer Groups close to the coast so we could throw the allies back into the sea as soon as they landed. I objected. The risk was enormous. We had such an inadequate force. It was safer to hold the Panzers in reserve and not commit them until we knew where the landing was for sure. I kept thinking that there would be more than one landing. And that they would need a port. It ended up being a moot point as we knew they were coming and there was nothing we could do about it. Hitler came to Soissons and had a meeting with Rommel and myself. We all saw the situation a little differently. During the meeting there was an air raid and we had to take shelter in a bunker. Hitler never liked to face reality that did not fit in with his plans and Rommel and I had just given him a bleak picture. He had not liked what he heard and could not wait to return to Berlin. We had to stand together for an hour in the darkened shelter. It was especially uncomfortable in the light of a conversation I had with Rommel earlier. Rommel had finally convinced himself that Hitler was intent on destroying Germany and he had joined the conspiracy to kill Hitler and he, Rommel was to head the new government.

"I remember telling Rommel that we were soldiers, not revolutionaries. But still he went ahead with the plan. I sometimes think that his death was more honorable than my life."

Rundstedt halted again and a glazed look came into his eyes. He was seeing a future for himself that he had never imagined. He shuddered involuntarily.

"After the invasion and the Allies made the breakout and the Falaise pocket collapsed, I called Keitel, who had managed to make himself Hitler's number one yes man. Hitler must have been in the room with him as there was a pause after all of my comments, as if Keitel was repeating them to someone else. I told him of the collapse of our army at Falaise and that the Americans had installed Patton to exploit the breakout. Patton was the one American general that we feared. What should we do? Keitel asked. End the war, you fools, was my reply. The line immediately went dead and two days later von Kluge arrived and told me he was my replacement. The war went on for another year.

"That was July of 1944 and a few days later the aborted coup took place. Hitler managed to live through an explosion that should have killed him. This time my retirement was short lived. It was not a pleasant time."

Blumentritt switched off the tape recorder. "I understand, my General. There is no need to go into all that."

Rundstedt's eyes flashed. "Of course there is. We will go through everything.

"After this attempt on Hitler's life I was appointed to head the Court-Martial that was to dismiss all members of the

Army from the service so they could be tried by the people's court in Berlin. General Beck committed suicide and the Gestapo found his diary which implicated all the officers, by date and name, who were involved. The height of stupidity. Goebbels was right. Revolutionary amateurs.

"I thought it was better for me, who loved the army, to head this court. If the evidence was not in black and white then the charges were dismissed and the officer was returned to duty. Many were killed but many were saved also."

Blumentritt managed a weak smile. "And myself. I was guilty of the same treason. But I was never caught."

Rundstedt had to laugh. "We always knew that Himmler was not the brightest of men. He actually helped von Stauffenberg with the satchel that contained the bomb and after it went off he tried to arrest the construction workers."

They both laughed.

"Let me add a few words about the conspiracy. I was never part of it and I silenced all talk of treason in my presence. I was still under the influence of Luther. The state could do no wrong. But Hitler could be resisted and if the generals could have presented him with a united face we could have changed things. Hitler was mad but he was also a political animal. He had the Chancellorship legally, and he could have been stopped legally. But he outsmarted us. He appealed to personal ambition and the general staff was all too prone to this divisiveness. But you were right when you pinpointed 1938. If we had stood behind Fritsch and taken a firmer stand."

Rundstedt looked around the room eerily. "The world would be a much different place today."

Kurt scowled and stood just inside the kitchen door. A clap of thunder sounded in the distance while a fine driving rain fell against the window. A small tree which grew in the yard beat its branches on the paned windows which lined the walls of the kitchen. The staccato tapping of the branches accentuated Kurt's remarks.

"Little Mary Sunshine, that's what you are. I am more like today; grey, wet and damp. The weather of despair. I will admit something to you. I am attracted to you. But only that. Like the whores during the war. All of these empty places inside of me. I will not let them be filled. I have this guilt I carry around with me like a sack of bricks. All those Jews and Poles and Gypsies. I can't stop thinking about it. I can't stop remembering. You know where I go on holiday? I go to Dachau. There is a museum there now. Immediately when you enter the room you see an immense photograph showing two Jews hanging by their arms which are tied behind their backs. You can see how painful it is. Their arms will be dislocated and they will never be able to use them again. Two guards are standing in front of them, smoking and laughing. Why are they torturing them if they are going to die anyway? And then I think that the guards do not care. They are like guards anywhere, just following orders. It is the same thing, I think to myself. But I know it is not the same. I am living in this half world of terror and insanity. I must be able to have it make sense. When our generals upstairs feel bad because things go wrong I have no sympathy for them whatsoever. They put themselves in the driver's seat. They were arrogant enough to think they could direct affairs. Or when natural disasters decimate cities and towns, it is easy for me to deal with these things. But the full extent of the outrages of the Nazis that were perpetuated on the Jews and Gypsies I can not handle. I saw it happening. I have adapted every point of view imaginable and I can still not live with it. For starters, every Jew in the world would be killed and when all the Jews were gone then the Nazis would start on the next group of undesirables. There was to be no end to the killing. It was a way of life. And no one cared. Especially about the Jews. When I killed that SS man I thought that if just ten percent of the German nation did what I did the madness would end. But very few cared. When resistance appeared the SS and the party backed down.

"In Denmark the King insisted on wearing the yellow badge of the Jew and the Danes never collaborated. Comparatively speaking very few Jews were killed in Denmark. The same in Bulgaria where the King and the people refused to cooperate. Hitler and the Nazis could be resisted successfully. The British were beautiful. When the SS originally started to transport the Jews from Austria after the Anschluss, they wanted to send them to Palestine. The British answer was to restrict immigration into Palestine. The Americans were the same. They refused to accept a shipload of Jews into America because the papers were not in order. Then the American State Department issued a memorandum saying that the government will not communicate with individuals. This meant that the only official way the U.S. Government had of receiving news from Germany was from the Nazis themselves. Millions of people were murdered and no one ever said to Hitler that you must stop this. You think that now the horror is ended? Now it just starts. Fifty years from now all anyone will remember is how close they came. They will note the Nazi tactics and they will employ them and they will copy their successes. Everyone is looking at 1945 as the end of something horrible and perverse in the world. I see it as a beginning; this is my curse." Kurt stood and stared out at the rain.

"Curse or no curse, lunch is ready." Anna took Kurt by the arm and led him to the table. "Tomorrow in the afternoon while the generals nap we will take a ride into town and meet a man there. They are almost finished. You will be leaving the day after tomorrow."

"Almost finished. Almost finished." Rundstedt said a few times. Then he took up his narrative again. After the Court-Martials were finished in August of 1944 I was returned to my command in the West. Hitler was running out of generals. From then on the orders coming out of the Supreme Command resembled a conversation from the Mad Hatter's tea party. I had occasion to visit Hitler's headquarters from time to time and it was madness elevated into a fine art. I was in the anteroom with General Model who was then commanding Army Group North. We could hear Hitler screaming at Keitel and Jodl. What is happening? Who is sending us these lies? Aachen. The American army is in Aachen. This is too much. Lies. If the American army is in Aachen why are we not attacking? There would be silence and the door would open. Keitel would motion for Model to enter and as Model entered Keitel would whisper, Attack Aachen. Then Hitler would shout at Model. What is happening on your front? What are your plans? Model would reply, My Fuhrer, I plan to attack Aachen. Then Hitler would calm down and smile at Model. Model was made a Field Marshal before the war ended. That was the only way to deal with Hitler in those days. On the day of the invasion we lost almost 24 hours in moving the Panzers into Normandy because Hitler was sleeping. No one had any authority to move any units except Hitler. He could not get to sleep and he would finally fall off at about dawn and the day of the invasion he slept until the afternoon. No one dared to awaken him so by the time the order to move the Panzers was given we had lost a complete day.

"What fooled me the most during that invasion was the Americans bringing their own harbor with them. I was certain they would need Cherbourg or Le Havre or Calais to embark their equipment. They floated their own harbors with them and were able to land at low tide. Remarkable. Then there was Hitler's last gasp attack through the Ardennes in December of 1944. It was called the Rundstedt offensive, so when it failed it would not have Hitler's name associated with it. I had a meeting with him just prior to the offensive. He admired me, he said. He knew I was not a Nazi and that I did not agree with the principles of National Socialism. But that did not matter. He knew I was a good German and I would do my duty. If it were not for my age he would have made me his

Commander-in-Chief long since. After leaving this meeting I was extremely depressed. Hitler prevented me from raising any objections to the attack. He wanted to get to Antwerp. The Panzers ran out of gas on the other side of Bastogne. That was the end of our last offensive. Militarily it hastened the end. I imagine we frightened some American generals badly. I often thought that if the British and American generals had nerve and a sense of history, a flair for the perfect attack at the perfect time, they would have turned Patton loose and let him come right into Germany through the same Ardennes. That would have been the end for us right then. And what poetic justice, eh Gunther?"

Blumentritt nodded and smiled.

Chapter 6

The house was quiet and the sun had reached its zenith as the low gray clouds broke up and patches of blue sky appeared. Kurt pulled the Mercedes around to the front of the house and Anna got in. They drove into the resort town and they stopped in front of a small watch repair shop on a side street, only two blocks from the square.

A bell tinkled when they entered. The shop was cluttered with old boxes and packing crates. There was a work bench surrounded by a small brass cage. A high stool sat in front of the bench. Outside of the cage were two threadbare chairs. Kurt and Anna sat down and waited. A grandfather clock made its presence known by tolling the quarter hour. The only light in the shop came from the street, and after a few minutes a gnomish figure emerged from the darkness in the rear of the store. The figure clicked the light on over the work bench and peered out at them through the bars of his brass cage.

"Oh, my dear Anna. It is you. Excuse me, please, my eyes...let me put on some tea. What, another package? Angel in heaven. More strudel...Aah...I shall die."

He came around from behind his cage and took the package that Anna offered him.

"Excuse me, sir...Leo...my name is Leo." He stood a respectful distance from Kurt, and when Kurt stood up and shook his hand he appeared to relax a bit.

"Here, here," Leo said as he busied himself behind the cage for a moment. "I have some water on. Tea, or coffee? No, it's no trouble. Here..."

Leo cleared a space on the counter and set out an ancient silver tray which held three American plastic cups, three lumps of sugar and two small containers, one with tea and the other with coffee.

"You will have some of Anna's strudel. What, you have been eating her cooking? Impossible. You don't look fat enough."

They all had a short laugh.

Anna asked of Leo, "Please if you don't mind. I keep thinking how painful it must be for you. Perhaps you could tell Mr. Eber here of your experiences since you left Poland in 1939."

"Ach, my dear. I would be glad to. No, there is no pain in the memory. Not any more. It is like someone who finds out he has cancer. At first, it is dreadful. And then, what can you do?"

Leo talked like any of a million European Jews. His hands were constantly in motion, reaching out to touch you as he made his points, describing fantastic patterns in the air. His eyes were sunk deeply into his head, and he seemed to be always on the verge of tears. His shoulders were constantly shrugging, and his arms would stretch out into the air, palms up. His speech was full of the expressions of his past.

"I should lie to you? You shouldn't have this happen to you. I should not lie to you?"

Even his declarative statements came out like questions.

"How could I tell you?" he started, looking directly at Kurt. "Who could believe the things I saw, the things I have done? A man was here last week. I am a writer, he said. I will write your story so the world would never forget. I laughed. Listen, I said to him. You are a writer? If you were ten Bernard Shaws and ten Leo Tolstoys all put together you could not write the things I saw. Still I talked to him. Who knows, maybe he can say it. I don't think so.

"You know what hunger is? You think you know what it is like to be hungry? Here, look." Leo held up his hand. "An SS man at my camp, he said to a group of us, here Juden, here. An orange. What am I bid for this orange." Leo indicated his left hand which he still held in the air. His little finger was missing. "One man in our command said to the officer. 'Please sir, don't kid with us. Why would you want to fool us. An orange. You know we have nothing of any value. A hat, my shirt. You want my shirt?' It was a fine clear day and the SS was in a good mood. 'Come, come Juden. Surely you have something you would give, something that would be worth this orange.' I came forward then when I could see that he was not just fooling around. He was ready to give his orange away if we could please him. If you give me that orange I will give you my finger. I said it very calmly. I was not crazy. I knew this SS. That's right, I repeated. I will give you my finger. I held out my hand to him. Go ahead, pick one. You can have any one that you want. Two fingers? You want two fingers? Fine, I will give you two fingers. Then the SS saw that I was serious and called over one of the guards and another SS officer. Give him your knife, the SS said to the guard. The guard handed me his knife. A large well-sharpened hunting knife like the kind you see in the movies. I said to myself, how simple this will be and I will have an orange. I laid my hand down on the ground and cut off my little finger with one quick stroke. The guards and the SS laughed and the SS threw me the orange. I wrapped my bleeding hand in a piece of my shirttail. And I ate my orange. The rest of my command was mad with me. They were mad because they didn't think of it first."

Leo paused as he stirred his tea and helped himself to some of Anna's strudel. "I would do it again." Leo laughed. "I have never missed my little finger. I do not think I would have survived that winter without that orange. It was 1942 and I was in Maidanek. So who would believe? You can get hungry. See how hungry you can get?" Leo smiled.

"And you think to yourself that life is so important? It is not true. Sometimes there are things more important than life. Once, in Maidanek also, there was a guard. A fat, preposterous Ukrainian, a real sadist. He would hit you on the face, smack. Like that with his stick. For nothing. And it was always dangerous to be hit on the face, because if you were bleeding or scarred in any way, then during the selection you would be picked for the morning killing. So after two or three months I developed a real hatred for this guard. And one day he ordered me to pick up some stones that were in the path by the barrack where we lived. Just that same morning I had seen him hit a young girl in the face with his stick. He broke her nose and she cried so pitiably. It was, how should I say, it was all so senseless. She was going to die anyway. When he shouted at me 'Juden,' I did not stop. He ran after me. 'Juden, I called,' he said.' 'So?' I said to him. 'Pick up those stones.' He poked me in the ribs with his stick.

"Something came over me then. 'No,' I said. 'I will not. You're an evil and filthy brute. I will do nothing for you.'" Leo laughed at himself. "Imagine, little me in that Hell, all of a sudden I single out this guard as being evil." Leo chuckled again. "Some Germans were passing then and they stopped. 'What is the trouble here?' The German wanted to know. 'This Jew refused to obey an order.' The guard couldn't wait to blurt it out. He was waiting for the Germans' permission to kill me. At that time it was great sport for the Germans to have the prisoners hacked to death with a shovel. I cannot describe it. I saw it many times and it is beyond my description. But the Germans felt it would put fear in our hearts. They could not threaten us with death, but they could threaten us with a particular type of death. Being hacked to death, alive, with a shovel, certainly put fear into us. All I could think of was that this German would laugh and tell the guard to hack me to death with a shovel, like my friend Moshe. He lived through three years of the camps with me, and then he was killed with a shovel in the streets of Lublin.

"But let me finish. I am interrupting myself." Leo paused. He looked around as if someone had stopped him from continuing his narrative.

"So the German says to me, 'What is wrong, Juden? Do you want to die?' and I shook my head at him. 'No', I said. 'No, I don't want to die. But this guard,' I pointed at the Ukrainian. 'I hate him so. I will die rather than do what he says. Go ahead, kill me. I will not obey this man.' Only I didn't say man. I think I said pig. In any event I meant it. My life that day was not as important to me as my hatred of that guard."

Leo laughed again. "Well, obviously I did not get killed. The German laughed. He thought it was very funny. He sent the Ukrainian away and he and his friends thought it was a grand joke. Thank God," Leo paused and looked upward.

"Thank God." He repeated. "I was transferred soon after that or that guard would have killed me for sure. So you can see that life is not as important as you think it is."

Leo paused for a moment and Anna and Kurt drank their coffee. Leo sipped on his tea and when he put his cup down his hand was shaking. He smiled. "You see, still today, almost ten years later, I still get upset thinking about it." Leo arose and disappeared into the back room for a moment. He reappeared and took up his narrative again.

"And another thing about life that I am still not able to understand. Food can be so important when you are hungry all the time. Here, here is another small episode. Believe me when I get going I could talk your head off. I was in Thereinstadt for a while. That was a camp in Czechoslovakia. As camps went, Thereinstadt was the Ritz. The SS maintained Thereinstadt as a kind of show place. Red Cross packages were allowed there. Mostly political prisoners and a work force for the factory that was close.

"But even there the killing went on. Each morning a selection was made and fifty Jews were shot. Every group in the camp had worked out an elaborate ritual for the portioning out of the bread ration. Food was so important and hunger was the motivating force for everything. Each group would select one man from among them. It was a Rabbi if you were fortunate enough to have a Rabbi in your group. If not, then the holiest and most trusted man in the group was chosen. When the bread ration arrived this person would take it and cut it into equal shares and everyone would stand with their backs to the man doing the cutting so they could not see him. Then he would pass out the ration and everyone would eat fast and not dare to look at anyone else's portion. You see, you go so crazy from hunger that no matter how equally the bread was cut, no matter how even the shares, you would imagine that the other person's share was larger than yours. In the beginning before this technique was worked out men fought to the death over such matters. But now it was a normal routine. If you never saw the other person's share it was better. Believe me.

"One morning after the selection had taken place and we were waiting in front of our barracks, the squad of soldiers who were to do the shooting was late. The men who were to be shot that day were standing, waiting in the compound. From our vantage point we could see through the fence into the shooting compound. There was a large ditch there and a sulfur fire was burning in it at all times. Those who were shot would fall into the ditch and their bodies slowly consumed by the burning sulfur. While we were waiting the daily bread ration arrived. Besides the portion for our group the guards also had the portion for the men who were to be shot. Give us their portion, we pleaded. They will have no need of it. But the guards were heartless and insisted on carrying out their orders to the letter. They gave the portion to the group condemned to die. Now this is the unusual thing. We watched them through the fence. While the execution squad was marching into the compound the condemned men went through the same routine. One man cut the bread while the others stood with their backs to him. And they were to die in less than five minutes."

Leo acted out the actions in pantomime so Kurt and Anna could better understand him. He was standing with his face to the wall and his back to them. "Imagine." He said. "Could you believe it?

"So you should know from this that there are some things more important than death even." Leo paused and shook his head.

"You want to hear more? I am not boring you? Even in my youth, in Poland in the early thirties my mother would say to me, Leo, she would say, you are a born story teller. I was a regular, how should I say it? Even then I was a regular gossip. I could never shut up.

"When the Germans first came to our little town in Poland we didn't know what to think. They can't be worse than the Poles, we all thought. The Poles, they really hated the Jews. And first the army, the German army came through our town. They all had such magnificent uniforms. And they were so clean. Things must get better for us. We were so poor, us Jews in Poland. We were the poorest people in the world. We had nothing. Four and five of us living in one room. What could the Germans want from us? We were so poor. They were such a strong and prosperous nation. Perhaps they would teach us how to be prosperous too.

"Don't shake your head. We thought like that at first. Then one of the soldiers said to me one day. 'Juden, if you value your life run away from here. You will all be killed.' 'No,' I said. 'Why would anyone want to kill us?' And the soldier told me to watch out. 'See, we have the Eagle here, on the left front of the uniform. When the soldiers arrive who have the bird here,' and now he pointed to his arm, 'then you will see.'

"I did not believe him. Very few of us believed him. And even if we believed him where were we to go? Where in the world were we to go in Poland in 1939?

"Sure enough, two days later the soldiers with the Eagle on their arm arrived one morning. As I said, our town was so poor, what could they want with us? They put a machine gun at the end of the street and a squad of soldiers started to yell at us. 'Alles Juden. Runter. Alles Runter.' We were herded out into the middle of the street. Everyone in our little town. 'Achtung. Achtung.' The shouts continued. The first thing, anyone who resisted, so help me. Why should I lie?, anyone who resisted. Bang."

Leo pointed his finger. "Like that, so quick it was unreal. Bang. And they were shot in the head. Mrs. Berg, she was our village seamstress. She held a soldiers' arm for a second. She was standing next to me. And the soldier shot her in the face. I knew her well. She was not resisting. She was asking him a question and there she was dead in front of her own house."

Leo paused again and stared between Kurt and Anna. "I knew then we would all be killed. You could believe, I knew it then. Every Jew in Poland would be killed. So we stood in the middle of our own street. We were separated; women and children to the left; men to the right. And then another separation. The old, sick and infirm with the women and children. Then march.

"Off we went. My village, my wife and child. Friends and relatives. I have never seen any of them since. Much later I heard that the women and children were marched into the woods, dug their own grave and were shot that night. My wife and I had been married for only three years. Our child, my little joy..."

Tears were running freely down Leo's face but he was not crying. He was in control of himself except for the tears. "I cannot think of them at all anymore. And the time before that day, my life before then, I cannot remember at all. But I am getting away from my story.

"We were marched that night some twenty kilometers. We were all in good shape so this was not a bad march. Not like later, at the end, when thousands of Jews were literally marched to death, only days, or sometimes even hours, from freedom and liberation. But that night the march was nothing for us. We arrived at another larger town at dusk that day. We were sorted and classified by trade. Watchmakers were few and far between, and there were only a few of us from the four towns that were gathered there. We were immediately separated from the rest of the group. We had not eaten all day and we were hungry. It was the beginning of six years of hunger.

"I went to work in an armaments plant. We, my fellow watchmakers and I, were formed into a team and we assembled, and designed timing devices. Then the plant we worked for was shut down and we were re-settled. I was sent to Treblinka. But my profession saved me. No one ever left Treblinka alive. Yet I spent two days there. And that was before I went to Warsaw. For a while I worked for the Government-General in Poland. That was in 1940-1941 before the killing really started. Warsaw was bad in those days, but not that bad. We still had only premonitions of what was to come, of the catastrophe that awaited. But you should believe me, I did not care for the fate of the Jews. I did not even care for my own survival. All I could feel was this immense guilt because I was alive and my family dead. I lived two years with this guilt.

"Then a strange thing happened to me. I was going through life, since my wife and children were killed that night, like, how should I say, a Zombie. Then one day, I think it was in Maidanek, now you shouldn't believe me because I am not too sure, but it doesn't matter where, this shipment arrived. A young man, a man I knew from my village was on the shipment. He had lost his wife that same night as I in 1939, but he had a son who was older, a boy of perhaps fifteen or sixteen. They had stayed together for two years, one way or another. And now his boy was dead. He had been shot by an SS on the platform at Maidanek. My friend, Moshe, after almost two years. I was so happy to see someone from home. But he looked right through me. Yes, he remembered me and the town. His son was dead and he didn't care. As I said, he looked through me and his eyes had that look of someone already dead.

"I found out which barracks he was assigned to and I went there that night. It was a death sentence to be out after curfew so I made up my mind to spend the night there with him. Moshe was the first human contact I had attempted in two years.

"We talked, or I should say, I talked, for almost two hours. Moshe never said a word. Here me, I hadn't said five words to another person for two years and now I'm talking my head off to Moshe. Moshe just keeps staring at me with his dead eyes. Sometime after midnight I dozed off and when I awoke a few minutes later, Moshe was gone. Then I saw, so help me you should believe, Moshe was hanging by his neck just a few steps from where we were talking. I tried to lift him up and to undo the belt that was around his neck at the same time. But I was too clumsy. One of the other barrack inmates woke up then.

'What's going on?'

'Help me,' I said, 'he's hung himself.'

'Let him die. Let the Jews die in peace. We have a rule here. Anyone who wants to die can.'

"But the man came and helped me anyway. 'Praise the Lord,' I said. Because Moshe was still alive. And then I, you must believe this, I and this unknown Jew who was helping me in the dark, started to laugh. Thousands of Jews were being murdered every day in this hell hole and I was praising the Lord because one Jew was still alive. And we all knew it was just a matter of time. We were all going to die anyway.

"But that night we were both glad that Moshe was still alive. And from that night on I started to live again. I went through three more years of that hell. And do you know why? But first poor Moshe. I think I told you, poor Moshe was killed, hacked to death with a shovel by a Ukrainian in Lublin. And I stayed alive."

Leo paused and stared away from them with that same look in his eyes. It was impossible to look Leo in the eye for more than a few seconds at a time. His eyes were eddies, tiny whirlpools that were capable of drowning your soul.

"I used to think that I regained my will to live because I was going to be the witness. I was going to survive so that the world should know what happened." Leo shook his head sadly. "But believe me that is not the truth. There are so many witnesses. There is so much evidence. The Germans themselves kept such good records. They indicted themselves. I don't know why I'm alive. I forgot. You don't believe me? That you could forget such a thing." Leo paused again.

Kurt spoke for the first time. "Have you ever thought, if you had the power and you were the judge. What would you do?"

"Of course I dream of that. Many times I have that dream of having all the power and being the judge. But it is no good. To do to them what they did to us? To kill their wives and children, their little babies?" Leo shook his head for emphasis.

"No, never. I could not do that to them."

Kurt asked another question. "But what would you want? Surely you would want something."

Leo nodded his head. "Yes. I want everyone who did this to us should first, they should first admit it. They should say, yes, we murdered millions of Jews for no reason except they were Jews. And second they should say they are sorry.

That's all I want. That they should admit it and they should say they are sorry."

That afternoon Rundstedt appeared in his study in full uniform. His buttons were polished and his boots were resplendent. He saw the look on Gunther's face and he sat down. "I could not resist. I loved the army so much. I could not help myself." He smiled warmly.

"You know I had a dream just now before waking from my nap. It was that Polish family again, from 1939. The man, and the wife with the two children. I saw them again standing naked and defenseless in that field. The boy, fighting back his tears, and the man talking to him, and the boy, regaining his courage, and staring back across the field at the soldiers and the machine gun, keeping himself in front of his mother. I could see it all so clearly. And I realized something. A great question poses itself in my head. What could the father have said to the son at that moment? He was so calm, so dignified. What could he have possibly said? I wrack my brains and I cannot know what he would have said. And it is because of my arrogance. Gunther, to have true honor and dignity, one must have humility."

Rundstedt said this with a note of finality. There was silence for the longest time as Rundstedt organized his thoughts. Blumentritt moved uneasily in his chair.

"You remember, Gunther, how I told you about that day in my life in 1905. Since the war ended I have been making notes and collecting incidents to illustrate attitudes and points of view about the last twenty years. You remember how I had associated my God, the God of Martin Luther, with duty and honor. And how it was this steadfastness, this absolute obedience which, part and parcel with my honor, was cemented into the core of my existence. Well, everything has come together for me again. Just like that day in 1905 when I stood on the threshold of my career. Now, almost fifty years later, having achieved my life's ambition, having carried this same honor through two wars, having survived the holocaust of a shattering defeat, and earned the respect of my country's enemies and friends alike, I can say, unequivocally, it has all been wormwood and gall!"

Rundstedt arose and started to pace around his chair. "That's right, Gunther. It is ashes in my mouth. If only I had it to do over again. I was wrong, Gunther. And Germany, at its best was wrong, and horror of horrors, Martin Luther himself was wrong.

"Did you know Geloso, the Italian general? Do you remember the absolute contempt with which we held the Italian army? Did you know that Geloso had his soldiers protect the synagogue in Athens from an anti-Semitic mob? When a protest was made to the Chief-of-Staff of the Italian army about Geloso's pro-Jewish attitude do you know what the Italian general replied? He said, 'anti-Jewish excesses are not compatible with the honor of the Italian army.' A German historian who visited me while I was under detention in England told me that story. Then he said, 'a sentiment I wish had been expressed by a German general.'

"He was right, Gunther. The Italian army was a ragtag mob that was not capable of fighting its way through an army of deserters. They were disorganized and poorly trained, but they survived the war with honor. Something we Germans could not do.

"Don't you remember the incident at Annency, when the Italian army in France surrounded the local police and SS barracks and threatened to kill them all unless the trainload of Jews bound for Auschwitz were released? You must remember, Gunther. The complaint from the SS commandant, Knochen, came directly to you. And we replied, I believe, with some message like, the Italian army is only under our jurisdiction for purely military matters. And Knochen was furious. But we felt we had put one over on the Nazis. My God, Gunther. We didn't do anything. It was the Italians, not us.

"To return to my Polish family again. Right after the war

and for a few years thereafter, as the extent of the murdering became known, more and more Germans became more disillusioned with the Nazis and with themselves. With every revelation of the millions killed and how it was done, the suicide rate would go up all over Germany. But the numbers never meant anything to me. If I could find evil in the state for murdering one innocent family, I did not need five million more to bring the point home. This is where the reality of evil escapes us so often. It seems to be axiomatic to the modern world that there is an acceptable rate of sin. At first the Murder Squads killed only sporadically. The Jews in Warsaw were willing to accept the most dire conditions as long as some of them were allowed to live. They revolted when it became apparent that the Nazis intended to kill them all. We are all prepared to live with some horror from our government. When it accelerates and the numbers get too large for us then we are ready to revolt and force a change. But the sin, the evil is sufficient and unchanging. The law is simple enough. Thou shalt not kill!"

Rundstedt collected his thoughts. "This is what that Polish family did for me. It allowed me to see the reality of evil and to realize that the state was wrong, and for a man to invest his honor in a nation or a state, was for a man to lose his honor completely. Contrary to Luther's views a nation or a state is Godless."

Blumentritt looked around the study and then back at Rundstedt. "This is absurd. What good can possibly come of thinking these things in this manner? Everything has already happened. The victories that we won are ours forever. The dead are dead. Nothing will change that."

Rundstedt spoke on as if Blumentritt had never said a word. "Some day soon now I will walk into our little town. I understand there is a Jew there, old before his time who lost everything to the Nazis. I will apologize to him for myself and the German nation and then ask for his forgiveness. A small act you think? Perhaps. But in the eyes of God it may buy me some salvation. That's the promise in the belief. I have come to the conclusion, you know, the inscription on the belt buckle of the German army, God with us. And isn't this the same God that the Hebrews gave to us? God was there all through the war. At Auschwitz and Buchenwald, at Sobribor, Chelmo and Treblinka. And as the ancient scripture has always taught us... I'm sorry if I am being incoherent. I can see so clearly now."

Tears were in Rundstedt's eyes and Gunther Blumentritt looked away, embarrassed for his general. Rundstedt remained oblivious to Blumentritt's embarrassment. He arose and went to the window and looked out at the field of flowers.

"Schema Yisrael," he said, as he repeated the ancient prayer in flawless Hebrew.

Kurt Eber packed the bags and was loading them into the rear of the Mercedes. A grey mist hung in the air and the morning dew imparted freshness to the world. Anna came out then and put a small suitcase and her coat on top of Kurt and Blumentritt's luggage.

"What is this?" Kurt was taken aback.

"I thought I would go to Berlin with you. I have a holiday. My cousin is coming this afternoon to look after the house."

She said this quite casually, as if she were commenting on the weather. "You have no objection to giving me a ride? I have already inquired of Herr Blumentritt."

"Of course. Of course." Kurt was flustered. "I mean, where will you stay? Isn't this rather sudden?"

Anna smiled at him. "If I can't stay with you, then I shall get a room somewhere."

Kurt slammed the lid of the trunk shut. "What are you talking about?"

"I told you Kurt. We should be married, you and I. It is no longer possible for me to have any children, but we can adopt some. There are still so many orphans from the war in need of a home."

Kurt looked at her and was unable to say anything.

Anna continued. "We must not forget why we are living. I need to be useful, to be caring for someone. And you need someone to care for you." She got into the front seat and rolled down the window.

Rundstedt and Blumentritt came out then. The Field Marshal kissed Anna on the cheek and shook hands with the two men. Kurt and Blumentritt got into the car and they left Rundstedt there with his flowers, his military music and his collection of uniform buttons. That same year he died, the book was published and it contained no mention of Rundstedt's innermost thoughts or confessions. General Blumentritt was convinced it was for the best.

Kurt and Anna were married in the spring of 1953.

www.ingramcontent.com/pod-product-compliance
Ingram Content Group UK Ltd.
Pitfield, Milton Keynes, MK11 3LW, UK
UKHW040558210726
13854UKWH00008B/1490

9 781425 161569